BOUND BY
BIRTHRIGHT

JANEAL FALOR

BOUND BY BIRTHRIGHT
Janeal Falor

ISBN-10:0-9897432-7-6
ISBN-13:978-0-9897432-7-3

To learn more about this author, please visit: www.janealfalor.com

Cover Photo by Damonza
www.damonza.com

Print Interior by Write Dream Repeat Book Design LLC
www.wdrbookdesign.com

First Edition
10 9 8 7 6 5 4 3 2 1

books in the
ELVEN PRINCESS SERIES

Bound by Birthright
Bound to Endure
Bound by Love

OTHER BOOKS BY JANEAL FALOR

MINE SERIES
Mine to Tarnish (Mine Prequel)
You Are Mine (Mine #1)
Mine to Spell (Mine #2)
Mine to Fear (Mine #3)
Sacrifice of Mine (Mine #4)

DARKENING LIGHT
Ever Darkening (Darkening Light #1)
Savage Light (Darkening Light #2)

For Karen
Thank you for always believing in me

Chapter
ONE

෴

SWORD FIGHTING is my favorite part of the week. I wish I got to do it more often, but mother barely lets me get away with what I'm already doing. She says an elven princess doesn't have the need for sword fighting. Despite not having the need, it's a passion of mine.

The room is full of guards watching me fight my sword master. The highlight of the month. It's been a tough fight, but so far, I'm winning.

I thrust my sword upward to block my opponent, but fail when a loud crash comes behind me.

"You have to learn to stay focused on the fight, no matter what," my sword master says, always teaching, even though I best him more often than not these days.

With a glare at my almost-nicked arm, I start to turn, to see what the commotion from that crash was about. Before

I can, someone dives at me from the side and knocks me to the ground. I squirm under the bulk.

"Stay here, my lady," a guard says, before pushing his weight off of me.

I grab my fallen sword and jump to my feet. The room has shifted from the guards watching me practice to chaos. My guards and sword master have surrounded a wild-eyed elf who brandishes two swords. I itch to join them, but hold back as I was instructed.

"Put it down," my sword master says. "We will spare your life if you turn yourself in."

"*Never*," the elf screams. He spins until we make eye contact, sending a jolt of fear tumbling through me. "She must die."

Something twists inside me as my sword master replies, "You know we won't let anything happen to Princess Arabella. Put down your sword."

"*No*. We will never allow the joining of humans and elves. We won't have that human scum become our king." The elf attempts to spring for me, but a guard blocks him.

"She must die!" He lunges for me again and is stopped once more, but this time my sword master butts him on the back of his head with the hilt of his sword. The crazed man collapses in a heap.

The guardsmen tie him up and haul him out of the room, still unconscious.

I can't believe what I just saw. Mother and Father warned me I was in danger, but I never accepted it. Never thought someone would try to take my life in earnest. It's hard to do anything but stare at where the crazed man fell.

While the three remaining guards secure the area, my sword master sheaths his sword and walks over to me. "Are you all right, my lady?"

"A trifle startled is all."

"Good. If I may make a suggestion, why don't we escort you to your quarters, where your servants will attend you?"

I nod. He holds out his hand for my sword. "I can take that for you."

I forgot I was still holding onto it. After reluctantly handing it over, I follow my guard to my quarters. The closer we get, the more my guards multiply. Word of the assassin must have spread. Once we get to my rooms, two of the guards enter first and check to make sure they are clear. Then I'm allowed to follow. My head servant, Constance, is waiting for me, as always.

"I heard what happened. Shall I have a bath drawn?" Her voice soothes me. She's taken care of me ever since I can remember.

"That would be fine." More than fine. Exactly what I need, to ease the tension from my muscles.

I breeze through the receiving room to my bedroom. A few steps in, I realize two of the guards have followed me. They've never before entered my room while I'm in it.

"Are you afraid someone got here before us?" I ask.

"We've been told to stand guard at your windows, my lady," the taller one replies. "Seems the attempted assassin scaled the wall and was able to enter the training room that way."

"I see." Grateful there are no windows in my bathroom, I change my path that way.

I enter, loving the smell of roses—my favorite scent. Constance directs the elf maid and the plump human one to fill the tub. Good. They always do a fine job.

I focus on my human servant. I haven't known many humans. There are always so many different things being said about them, but I don't know if they are true. I hope they aren't. This servant, at least, has never shown any indication of being cruel. She doesn't have the pale, fair skin of the elves, nor the ears pointed so fine they become almost like a strand of hair. Our ears are shapely and pert; hers are round and—I hate to say it, but—boring. Human ears.

It's because of her kind my life is threatened. Or rather, my soon-to-be joining of her kind. My upcoming marriage to a human.

Constance helps me out of my things. She puts a steadying hand on my trembling arm. When did I start shaking?

"I've had the girls throw some calming herbs in your bath."

"Thank you, Constance. I suppose I'm still surprised. I never thought anyone would want to hurt me."

"The queen and king have been warning you for months now. Though I hate to see you come to the truth of it this way." Constance clucks as she starts on the laces on the back of my dress. "There's a council meeting planned for this afternoon. I'm guessing they'll want to talk to you."

I sigh. Whenever they talk to me, it's to tell me what to do. Last time was what started this mess. My betrothal.

After my servants are finished, I slip into the tub. Constance washes my hair, and I can't tell whether she's using magic to soothe my nervousness or if it's the herbs. Maybe a bit of both. Either way, my muscles relax.

Constance was right. After my bath and a light lunch, I'm summoned to the throne room. I leave my servants to clean up, wishing Constance could come with me.

As if she knows what I'm thinking, she gives me a tight-lipped smile. "We'll be here when you get back."

I nod. She's always near.

My usual guard has doubled. I know I should feel protected, but all I feel is claustrophobic. The tight press of elves in full battle armor, clanging down the hall, makes me want to scream for space. Instead, I hold myself proper as a good princess should, just as my mother taught.

We approach the throne room, and I run my hands down my dress to smooth it. After what's happened, I don't feel at all presentable, but nothing is amiss. I nod to the guard who opens the door for me.

The council room is quieter than usual. There are no assistants or note takers hustling about, just a handful of my parents' most-trusted advisers. They're chiefly older male elves who have been in my parents' service since before I was born.

The door closes behind me without any of my escorts following. This surprises me. Then I spot Stewart, the head of the guard, in a corner. He's older, almost a father figure to me, his dark hair silvering around his thinly pointed ears. He bows to me, as does everyone else in the room except my parents.

Mother's sapphire eyes shine with unshed tears, and mine prickle in response. I wave at the others to be seated, then take my place on the right side of my father, opposite my mother. My trembling legs getting a break make me grateful I don't have to continue to stand. I look down and blink rapidly to dry my eyes. Drawing from years of lessons, I steady myself and wait.

"Thank you for joining us," Father says, his hands latched together. "We have been discussing the attempt on your life earlier today. You are this kingdom's most prized possession."

"I'm not sure I qualify as the most prized. There are other—"

"Enough, child." At his stern rebuke, my cheeks flame. I keep my head up but don't meet the gazes of any of the council as my father continues. "You are our most prized possession, and as such, your safety requires everything must and will be done to guarantee it."

"I still say this isn't the right answer," says Reginald, Octavian's assistant, in his nasal tone.

An elf slams his fist on the table closest to me. "What would you have us do?"

I glance at him.

Octavian's massive girth occupies the chair. His jowls shake as he continues. "It's either this answer, or one of the assassins will be able to carry through with their plot."

"Agreed," a skinny elf named Oscar replies.

"Silence." Father's voice is quiet but still heard above the din. "We've already agreed to act. There will be no more squabbling in front of my daughter." He turns to me, face set but eyes betraying a hint of sadness. "Arabella, we have decided it would be best for your safety if we sent you into hiding. A few servants and Stewart will go with you. A decoy will be left here at the castle, and several more will be sent into hiding at other locations. Our hope is this will keep you safe until the wedding."

Hiding? My heart pounds. Is it really so serious? Forcing a mask of calm on my face, I ask, "When am I leaving?"

"Straight from here. Stewart has already made arrangements."

I'm not sure what this means for me. Whatever it is, it's not good. Surely there is a better way. But I nod my acquiesce.

"Good." Father turns back to the council. "You are dismissed."

The council members stand, bow, and chatter with one another as they leave the room.

On his way out, Reginald skirts the room to talk to me. "I will be wishing for your safety, my lady."

What a thing to need good wishes for. "Thank you."

He bows and trails the others out of the room. Once they are all gone, Mother waves me over. I kneel in front of her, and she folds one of my hands between hers.

"I shall miss you, Arabella." A few tears escape her eyes, wetting her smooth skin. Mother always looks perfect, and her tears somehow manage to make her more so. It is one skill she has not been able to teach to me, though people say I have inherited her beauty.

"I will miss you too," I say.

"You may be going into hiding, but remember you are still royalty. I expect nothing less. Stay safe while I make your wedding plans. I will have to manage without you. I'll make certain it is a grand event, worthy of my daughter."

I hold back a smile. She always manages without me. There's one thing I won't miss—not having to listen to all the wedding plans. I really don't care. I turn to Father, my hand still clasped between Mother's.

"My child." He smooths my hair as if I were still a girl. "I wish there was something else we could do. I hate to see you go. It is for the best, though. Keep that in mind while you're gone. This is for the best."

"Yes, Father."

He pats my head again. I have an urge to hug him, like I did when I was little and could get away with such a show of affection. Instead, I stand, as do both of my parents. Stewart walks over, a cloak in his hand.

"Take care of her," Father says.

"Yes, Sire." Stewart hands the cloak to me. "After you put that on, we will be leaving through a hidden passage. A decoy will exit this room in your place, so no one will suspect."

Wondering how they found enough girls to match my small stature, I drape the cloak around me, not used to doing so myself, and tie it. My mother gives my hand one last squeeze and my father nods, his sad gaze holding onto mine until Stewart turns and opens a secret panel.

I follow after him.

The panel slides shut behind me quietly and cuts out most of the light. Stewart leads me through several twists, turns, and stairways, sometimes turning down a new passage and sometimes skipping by a cross-section. Every once in a while, one of those new, fancy, electric lights shines in the hall, and I wonder who they got to hook it up if this way is so secret.

Stewart stops at each panel. He opens it, checks the passage it leads to and motions for me to enter.

I step in an unfamiliar room with another electric light and give a sigh of relief when Constance walks toward me with a dress in hand.

"We'll have her ready in just a minute," she says and hits something to close the panel. It's then I notice the two servants from earlier today are here as well. "Let's get you into something less noticeable."

They change my fancy dress for one like theirs, clean but simple. They quickly place my cloak back on and wash my face clean before they start on my hair. They unpin it, brush the curls that reach down to my waist, and braid them. They twist the braid around the back of my head and pin it up, not in an elaborate way like I'm used to but in a functional way like the servants sometimes wear their hair. After raising the hood of my cloak, they do the same with theirs. I look a lot like them.

"Is this enough of a disguise?" I ask.

"It's ample," Constance replies. "Your decoy will be moving about, and no one will be looking for you dressed as a servant in a group of servants heading out in the cold for a break."

Grateful I don't have to give away the trick I discovered with my magic some weeks ago, I say, "Good. Let's go."

Constance opens the secret panel to reveal Stewart waiting for me. We follow him down a few more twists and out a door that leads to the castle grounds. The garden is empty this time of year, though it's coming to life. Green is springing up everywhere.

While we head toward the servants' gate, Constance comes up beside me and loops her arm through mine. I startle at the contact. If it was anyone but Constance, I would pull away. Rarely does anyone besides Mother touch me.

Constance pats my arm. "All part of the act."

Stewart leads us through the gate, where no one gives us a second glance. Through the town we stroll, Stewart in front and two of my servants behind. It seems like a long time since I was in the council room with my parents, but I know it's not. Not long since my life was threatened. And according to them, not for the first time. This was just the closest attempt.

We come to a small boat, compared to what I'm accustomed to. It doesn't look like it will take more than Stewart and perhaps a few others to run it. There's a cabin for me to share with the female servants. After we all climb aboard, Stewart helps the crew of five men set sail.

As we drift away, I turn back toward the castle. It stands out from the rest of the city, up on the hill. It glistens in the sun, its white walls brilliant with plenty greenery growing on them. It's where I belonged until today. It's *home*. But I doubt I will see it again before I am to wed the human prince.

Chapter
TWO
~

SEVERAL DAYS LATER, I step onto a dock on Sulamay Island. It groans under my slight weight, and I hurry to the beach, grateful the dock didn't collapse under me and my pack. How will it fare under the weight of all the others? The girl servants, Constance, and Stewart are all staying.

The beach is sandy where the land meets the dock but turns rocky along the way. An overgrown rock path leads to a castle. It's sad looking—nothing like the clean, tall lines of home.

Constance comes to stand beside me. "It will work for a few months."

Am I really to be here that long? My heart already aches for home. "Since there is no other choice."

The crew and my servants, except for Constance, start hauling stuff into the castle. When they're done, they will leave. Having no escape from this island makes me feel claustrophobic, but they weren't paid to stay, only to bring us here. They think we are on a leave of absence that comes time to time for the best servants. I suppose my servants are pretty good, but I never thought of giving them a leave of absence. I couldn't afford to lose Constance even for a few days; no other servant is like her.

I wander up the path and through the open door of the castle. It's easy to tell where the servants have taken my things. A path of footsteps cuts through a layer of grime on the floor. I groan.

"We'll have it cleaned up in no time," Constance says, coming up behind me.

I hear a squeak, and a mouse darts through the entry hall. I look at Constance in disgust and say, "And I have every confidence that won't take long to get rid of."

"We should have brought a cat." She tries to smile, but it wavers to a grimace. "I hope Stewart doesn't mind catching rodent. Why don't you take a stroll outside until we can get this place clean?"

"Right. I'll be"—I have no idea where I'll be; I've never been here before—"around. I guess I can't get too lost on an island this size."

Constance nods, then sets off the way she does whenever she has a project to tackle. Remembering the mouse, I shudder and walk around the outside of the castle. Its stones are aged and crumbling in spots. It had better be sturdy enough for us to live in. Otherwise we'll be sleeping outside. Though with the condition it's in, perhaps that'd be a good thing.

The back of the castle is a different story. A comforting sight greets me—an enormous garden. Sure, it's overrun, but big enough I won't have to worry about what I'm supposed to do while I am here. I'll get my frustrations out on weeds. Unfortunately, my problems aren't as easy to pull out as they are.

A WEEK LATER, I'm out in the garden, enjoying the feel of the sun on my skin. The castle is cleaner, but I still prefer the garden. I run my fingers through the dirt. The hidden beauty has come alive under my care. The flowers are blooming, weeds are lessening, and an overall wild beauty shines out.

The human servant walks up to me. "Would you like some help, my lady?"

We haven't talked much in the last week. It's the least amount of conversation I've ever had, but my mother always discouraged too much formality with servants. "What's your name?" I ask.

"Jocelyn, ma'am." She shifts her weight from one foot to the other.

"Well then, yes, Jocelyn, help would be welcome. Start weeding over there." I point to the area I was going to work on next.

Jocelyn kneels down beside me and reaches for a not-yet blooming flower.

"Not that one. It will be a flower in another week or two."

Her cheeks redden. "Sorry, my lady. I thought everything here needed to be pulled."

Maybe she won't be as much assistance as I hoped for. "Here, let me show you," I say.

I spend the next half hour helping her distinguish which plants are to be kept and which are weeds. Most of that time I spend hovering worriedly, but she does fine after I show her.

I go back to my own area and find a sad-looking flower. I brush the wilting petals with the tips of my fingers and close my eyes. I pull at my magic, feeling it rise within me. Focusing only on the flower, I let the magic flow from deep inside me, through my fingertips, and into it.

The flower has been stifled too long by weeds and is weak. I push the magic further through the stem and into the soil, drawing nourishment into the plant. After pulling the magical fingers back inside me, I wipe my brow.

I sit back and open my eyes. The flower is perking up, the added nourishment doing its job. From the corner of my eye, I notice Jocelyn is staring.

I meet her wide, green-eyed gaze. "What?"

She looks down. "I'm sorry. I just never saw anyone use their magic like that before." She glances back up. "It was amazing."

My chest warms. "Thank you. I'm not surprised you haven't seen anything like it before. Elves having been using magic less and less lately. I think the new gadgets we've gained from the humans make it less needed. They don't have as many side effects."

"What do you mean by *side effects*?"

I pull at some weeds. "Everything in magic comes at a cost. For instance, I just pulled nutrients out of the soil, to help the flower. In doing so, I made the ground lose more nutrients than if the plant did it naturally, over time. I could just leave it, but then the flower would die. So later, I will go through the area I've worked magic on and add extra nutrients back into the soil. Compost or something. Sometimes Stewart does that part for me."

"I had no idea it could be so much work."

"I don't mind. Doesn't really seem like work to me. Plus it keeps my mind off things."

"Do you mean the death threats or your wedding? Death threats sound so horrid, but I can't even imagine marrying someone you don't love, let alone have never met. Why it seems positively ar—" Jocelyn stops, her hand hovering midair, with a weed still clutched to it, as I gape at her in shock.

"I'm sorry, my lady. Please, please forgive me." She drops to the ground on all fours and puts her head to the dirt. "I was out of place, Your Highness. I am so sorry."

I stare at her prostrate form, wondering what punishment would be fitting. I don't mind her words. Not really. It's nice to hear what someone really thinks for a change. But she is a servant. *Sigh.* "Get up."

She sits back up on her knees and brushes at the dirt on her forehead. Her gaze remains lowered to the ground.

"As punishment for your impertinences, I order you to work in this garden at least two hours every day, until we leave. And you get to do the compost when I finish tonight."

She wrinkles her nose. "Yes, ma'am."

I dismiss her with a wave of my hand, and she scrabbles back to her area. I slide over to a patch of shade. Lunch should be served soon, but hunger doesn't bother me; Jocelyn's words do. I was trying to keep my mind off all the people who want me dead.

Why would she think love matters? It's true I would like the opportunity to meet him, maybe get to know him a bit, before I have to spend my life with him. But love? Love is for those who don't have a duty to an entire nation. A duty to keep them safe. That's what this wedding is supposed to be—a joining of two nations, for trade and peace—but the threats on my life make it feel like the opposite is happening.

The hatred between humans and elves is building. I can only hope my marriage will help fix that. I lean against the tree and close my eyes. One nice thing about being in hiding—I don't have eyes watching me constantly, so it doesn't matter if I ease my posture for a bit.

SOMETHING WAKES me. I'm not sure what. I blink several times to clear the lingering blur of sleep. Jocelyn has a large pile of weeds next to her, but she's turned toward the castle, as if she heard something as well.

"Your Highness," my other servant, the plump elf one, yells. She bursts up the path and comes to a standstill in front of me, gasping for breath. "Ship coming... here soon... pirates."

I jump up and rush to the kitchen entrance, Jocelyn following. Stewart and Constance are waiting for me.

"What do we do?" I ask.

Constance looks at Stewart. "What do you think?"

"I don't know." He rubs his stubbly chin. "We could hide, but if they find us, they will know something is up, for sure. Her face is too well known. Even if they aren't looking for her, they will know who she is."

I hesitate, not wanting to give up my secret, but it's just for a moment. "I'll disguise myself."

"No offense, my lady," Constance says, "but it won't be enough. This isn't like keeping your head down on the boat. They will see past anything we do to cover up who you are."

"Not everything," I say.

I take a deep breath. The magic inside me grows, as I call it. I push it to my face and hair. A small cry escapes my lips, but I'm able to hold back my reaction to most of the pain. Increasing pigment to my hair is easy, but turning my blue eyes brown is much harder. Then I add a light dusting of freckles on my nose and cheeks. Once that is done, I focus on my ears. I pull the thinly pointed ears first into more of a leaf shape, and then all the way rounded, like a human's. I open my eyes and to find Constance's and Stewart's faces drawn with shock. Jocelyn and the plum human servant look pale.

"I discovered I could do it one day when I was bored," I rush to explain. "I can't seem to make myself look like anything but this yet. Not sure why it would be a human, but the pirates shouldn't recognize me. Right? You two don't recognize me, do you?"

Neither of them says a word; they continue to stare.

"Did I not do it right? Do I still look too much like myself?" I ask.

"No, dear. No, you don't look like yourself at all," Constance finally manages to say. "No, you don't look like yourself at all. I've never seen any magic like it."

This pulls Stewart from his stupor. "I haven't either. A few small changes here and there, but nothing of this magnitude. How much power do you have?"

I shrug. Maybe showing them wasn't such a good thing. "I'll change back, and we can think of a better plan."

Stewart holds up a hand. "No. Don't. This'll be the perfect thing to confuse the without us worrying about you getting recognized or making them suspicious."

"Are you sure? I know a couple places I could hide."

"Which might work, but we don't know how well they know this island. It hasn't been used much lately, so they may have made it some type of cache- or weigh-station. We can't know for sure. Hiding in plain sight will be much better."

"Do you know what the consequences are for this spell?" Constance asks.

I lower my gaze. "No. I haven't tried it that many times yet, and I never was able to determine what happened because of those times."

"If this wasn't an emergency, I would insist on you changing back." She clucks her tongue. "Not much we can do about it now. Where are we going to meet the pirates?"

Chapter

THREE

❦

A GIANT OF A MAN saunters down the gangplank
and onto the dock. It groans beneath his massive
weight, as if it's ready to fall apart. He gives it such
a look that I know the planks wouldn't dare do so and risk
his wrath. The human turns his attention on our small group,
huddled on the beach just off the dock.

I clench my teeth. Stewart said we should meet them down
here, like we have nothing to conceal. We should all have
hidden, whether I'm recognized as the princess or not. I've
seen this man's poster many times and heard of his heinous
crimes even more often. His gentlemanly coat and perfect
posture hide the ugliness inside him.

Maybe this was the only reason he stared. I don't let my
relief show. The group remains silent.

His towering frame looms closer. "Answer."

"We're both orphans," Jocelyn says. "Constance found us on Bardus when she was on leave."

I jerk toward her, then try to cover my surprise, hoping he didn't notice.

"And?" Captain Smythe leans closer to her.

"We were taken in and trained. Once we improved, we moved up in jobs, until we were able to earn leave and come here."

"I see." He pauses and then backs away from her and focuses back on the group. "My men and I have been traveling a long ways. I know elven food is heaven. You will prepare us a feast for this evening."

"We will prepare a simple meal," Constance says. "Since we are being generous and the princess is not here, you and your men will leave in the morning."

He makes his arm bulge, his hand forming a fist, and it vibrates as though he is restraining it. "We will have a deal if you also prepare three meals for us to take on our voyage."

Constance's eyes glow with anger. "I think we can arrange that. Should we start dinner now?"

"Yes. Get to work."

She lifts her eyebrows a bit in challenge, but turns and walks toward the castle. I follow, wondering how she still stands after all I've seen and heard about Captain Smythe. I'm grateful for whatever the reason is. The others rush after us, with Stewart protecting us at the rear.

Before we are halfway up the path, Captain Smythe calls out, "Wait. The humans stay with me."

The group halts. Cold permeates through me. He wants to see both of us, so he probably doesn't know about me.

What could he want, then? Those closed-door meetings flash through my mind, but I force them away. They are the last thing I want to think of right now. I want to flee, but it will only make things worse.

I force a feeble smile at the others, hoping they'll head back to the castle. We do not need to anger this man further than Constance already has.

They part, reluctantly. I stride toward him and grab Jocelyn's hand on the way. I'm not sure why I grabbed onto her, but it makes facing him again a little easier. The rest of my servants head back to the castle but slower than before and with many backward glances.

We stop a few feet from Captain Smythe, Jocelyn's hand trembling in mine. My heart is pounding erratically. I attempt to hide as much of my fear as I can.

He steps closer, and his hot breath falls across my face. He clasps my chin, confining me, but not as forcefully as he did with Jocelyn. My throat constricts as he moves my face from side to side, inspecting it. I squeeze Jocelyn's hand. She squeezes back. My spell is still in place. I triple check it, to be sure, but it doesn't ease my tension.

Finally, he lets go.

I rub my chin, feeling as if his fingers are still there. I have been trained to get a handle of any situation. He cannot best me. "What did you wish to speak of, Captain Smythe?" I ask.

His lips twitch into a brief smile, but he says nothing. His proximity is too much. I take deep breaths, but they don't work like they did before. Slowly, I shift my weight from one foot to the other.

He moves his gaze to Jocelyn. Though he now stares her down instead of me, I can't stop squirming. When she squeezes my hand, I squeeze back like she did for me.

Those thoughts, the times when court was held but I wasn't allowed to attend, keep coming, followed by the tortured elf I saw. These thoughts shouldn't be entering my mind, but I can't seem to stop them. I have to do something. I open my mouth to repeat the question since he ignored it, but approaching footsteps stop me.

I hold back a relieved sigh and turn to see who is coming. One of the crew members gallops down the path. His clothes are filthy and look even more so when he comes to a halt next to Captain Smythe. The smell that follows him makes me gag. I cough a few times, earning a dirty look from him, before he speaks.

"No sign of the princess in the castle or on the grounds. The royal chambers are in such a mess that one of our men was injured. A statue crashed on him while we were searching for hidden rooms or passages."

I smirk at the thought of one less pirate to deal with. Good thing I didn't hide, though. They don't sound familiar with this place, but they do sound thorough.

"Who?" Captain Smythe asks.

"James."

The captain grunts.

"He's being seen to," the other man says. "Nothing says she's here now or has been here recently. The servants' quarters are the only ones in use, and there is nothing in them to mean royalty would step foot inside them."

I try not to bristle. He's right, though. If Mother saw the accommodations, she might not have let me go into hiding. Or maybe she did know how bad they'd be and thought it worth the sacrifice. It would have been if I wasn't standing right next to a pirate intent on finding me.

"Not good enough. You were gone too short a time to do the job right. Tell half the men to search the castle and grounds again, doing a meticulous job, and tell the other half to search the rest of the island. She is here."

The crew member lowers his head, gives a nod, and retreats to the castle.

Captain Smythe looks back at me, and a tremor goes through me. "There's something different about you," he says.

Chapter
FOUR
❧

MY VISION sways.

"You girls are so different. It disgusts me."

The word *girls* eases me a bit—but only a bit.

His gaze travels between the two of us.

"It is revolting to see humans not just working with elves, but also serving them like common muck. Humans are better than that. Because you were taken away as children, I'll give you a second chance. Otherwise I'd slit both your throats right here."

Jocelyn wavers next to me. I can't bring myself to feel as scared as she looks. It sounds bad, but he doesn't know who I am, and slitting our throats would be an easy way out compared to what he could do. But what mostly represses my fear is the second chance. It had better be something I can work with and not another cruel step in his game.

"Ah. That gets your attention, doesn't it?" He grins, but his eyes grow dark. "When we leave tomorrow, you will both be on our boat, with all of your things. If we have to come get you, you won't be getting the second chance or an easy death."

He pivots and swaggers back to his boat. Once he's out of sight, I collapse on Jocelyn. Or maybe she collapses on me. One second, we are standing on our own, and the next we are only held up by each other in a shaking mass.

Though my feelings are a mess, I pull together before she does. "Come on. We'll be safer back with the others."

"There is no safety for us now," she murmurs.

I agree but say nothing. We let go of each other. I feel more vulnerable, but I don't grab onto her again. It was weak of me to do it in the first place—an act that doesn't bear repeating.

We scramble back to the castle. Danger tingles through me at the thought of the captain's demand.

We can't leave with him. I could send just Jocelyn, but I know he'd still come after me. I brush the thought away. I couldn't send Jocelyn even if it meant my own safety—which it won't. But if it did, I couldn't put her or anyone else in Captain Smythe's clutches. Our plans will have to be altered, but to what, I have no idea.

The door creaks as we enter through the main hall. It is no longer filthy, but not what I'm used to, either. Besides a few worn chairs, nothing is in the room. The smell of bread baking reaches me, coaxing me toward the oven.

I move through a couple halls and step into the kitchen. Constance looks up, her face momentarily relaxing before she looks back down at the meat she is working with. Sounds of something being shuffled about come in from the dining room. Emeline is working at the table, her gaze tense on us when we enter.

"Jocelyn, go fetch Stewart from the dining room and let him know you and Adelei have returned," Constance says.

"Yes, miss."

Jocelyn cuts across the room and leaves through the servants' entrance to the dining hall. A few seconds later, she returns with Stewart barreling in behind her.

"Are you all right?" he blurts out.

"Fine." For now.

"I wanted Stewart to come after you," Constance says, as she continues working with the meat. "He told me to give it a bit more time. What did Captain Smythe want?"

I sit at the table next to Emeline, who's working with dough and trying not to shake from fear. She halts her work while I talk.

"He said he doesn't care for humans working for elves, especially as servants, and that the two of us are to join him tomorrow, when he leaves."

Emeline punches the dough. A thump sounds to my side, and I turn to see that Constance has dropped the meat on the counter. She picks it back up and heads over to the fire pit. We all watch her try to put it on the spit, until Stewart helps her. Any relief that came at my return has vanished. A pall slips into the room. The echo of the pirates' footsteps moving about the castle, followed by a few vulgar words, make the gloom heavier.

"Work on your tasks and hope the intruders don't stay in the castle too long," Constance snaps.

Next to me, Emeline moves back to life. Jocelyn heads to the sink and begins working. How is it she knows what to do without being told? I've never before done anything in the kitchen, except for the times I snuck down for an extra treat when I was a girl. I'm long past those years, though, and I doubt that would help me blend in for the pirates.

Constance washes and turns around. She stops and tilts her head when she sees me. "Emeline doesn't need any help," she says. "Why don't you jump in with Jocelyn? She can show you what to do, in case a pirate walks in. Got that, Jocelyn?"

"Yes, miss."

"Is working only when they come around going to be enough?" I whisper just loud enough for Constance to hear me.

"It'll be fine. These scums probably won't notice if you do nothing, but we'll show you to be safe."

I nod, though the thought of helping out, even if it's only when one of the pirates comes in, fills me with almost as much nervousness as seeing Captain Smythe. If I can't do it right, I will be seeing him again in a worse way than before. Jocelyn shows me what to do, but it doesn't make any sense. My thoughts turn back to her words of marrying for love instead.

It's a nice thought, for commoners. For me, duty comes first. My people need something to help their relations with the humans, or war is sure to come. Humans are so arrogant, I'm not sure my marriage to a human will be enough to prevent it, and with Captain Smythe's demand thrown in, maybe my wedding won't happen after all.

I TAKE THE LAST bite of my portion of wild boar. The sweet, lightly nutty flavor fills my mouth. Delectable. Constance could switch to working in the kitchen back home, instead of staying with me. Life would be odd without her around, though.

If only one of us knew some way to poison the food, we wouldn't have to be dealing with the pirates anymore. But even with magic, none of us knows how to. If only magic was easier and without consequences, we could get out of this mess.

Light from a candle on the table flickers across my empty plate. The kitchen is growing chilly without the hearth lit. The spit hangs empty, the pirates having finished eating long ago what Constance didn't hoard for us. They don't deserve her cooking. I hope they choke on whatever they are still eating. I concentrate on the dining hall, trying to hear what's going on. I haven't been allowed in all night.

"Haven't had this good a food in a long while." Captain Smythe's compliment sounds odd after his earlier harsh demands.

"Aye. That it 'tis good, Cap'in," a sailor replies.

"Perhaps we should take the older one with us. I should be eating like this all the time."

"You'll leave me here, in peace." Constance's snippy voice disrupts the pirates' banter. The sound of a dish being slammed down halts any remaining conversations.

"What do you say to that, men? Should we leave her alone or not?"

My heart pounds. Another pirate speaks up, his speech slurring. "Don't thunk we wanna have anythin' so crabby as that, Cap'in."

The ruffians burst out in drunken laughter. There wasn't any alcohol in the castle until they brought their own from their ship. I want to curse its foul nature, but I can't help but hope it will provide us some means of getting out of this mess.

"The ravishing human maidens will join us in the morning, instead. Where are they, anyway?" Captain Smythe asks.

Jocelyn glances at me from across the table, and I sit up straighter.

"Attending to their duties," Constance says.

"Ah, well, they'll be around soon enough," Captain Smythe says. "They are mine. I'm not sharing this time."

"But, Cap'in, I wanna play with the bonny lasses, too."

The clink of glass breaking on the stone floor makes me jump. Constance had better control herself over its ruin.

"They're mine. Touch them, and I'll hang you from the yards," Captain Smythe roars.

Any desire to sneak a peek into the dining room is gone. My fear doubles in intensity, causing a physical pain in my chest.

I don't know how we can escape his demand. The plans he has for me as Adelei sound worse than if he took me for who I truly am. I'm not sure what he would do to me if he knew I was the princess, though. Either way, it isn't looking cheery. With a shudder, I stand to pace in the corner of the kitchen farthest from the dining room.

After a few minutes pass, I slow my pace. Jocelyn watches me from the table, playing with her silverware. My nerves continue to ease until another outburst from the pirates.

If only I could charge in there with my sword and take them all on. I would need a sword, though. Plus I've never been in a real fight, and with as many pirates as there are— some of them with guns—it would be futile. It would make me feel better, though.

Hearing the scuffle of chairs and moving feet, Jocelyn and I glance at the entrance to the dining hall. Only my servants have been in here so far, but I don't trust things to stay that way. The noise heightens then drifts away as the pirates begin to leave. After a few minutes, Constance comes through the door, followed by the rest of my servants. I come to a standstill, glad to see them but still wary of the shuffling going on in the next room.

"Captain Smythe is leaving early in the morning," Constance says. "He demanded his crew prepare the ship to depart. We are supposed to have their food ready before first light."

The sound of someone heaving reverberates through the room.

"Good riddance," I mutter, glaring toward the sound, but thankful I can't see the cause.

"We best get to work ourselves," Constance continues.

"Not that it'll matter much," Emeline mumbles then raises her voice. "We've all heard rumors about Captain Smythe. He'll get what he wants, even if he has to torture it out of us."

"We don't know that those rumors are true," Constance says. She must not have seen what I have. Lowering her voice, she continues. "I won't turn over the princess. Captain Smythe understands she's not here, and he's leaving to go look for her elsewhere. So far, they haven't shown the cruelty we've heard of. We can do this. We need to figure out how to help Jocelyn and Adelei out of going with him."

"I don't know, miss." Jocelyn puts her elbows on the table and her head in her hands, muffling her voice. "There's nothing that can save us from this."

Constance walks over and puts her hand on Jocelyn's arm. No one speaks. Jocelyn's shoulders start to shake with silent sobs. Emeline sits next to her and rubs her back.

I feel helpless. I can't order Captain Smythe to leave us alone.

The quiet is broken only by the occasional sound from Jocelyn. Constance and Stewart look deep in troubled thought. Emeline looks about to cry too.

The door to the dining room slams open, and a surprisingly sober pirate stands in the doorway.

"Just a reminder from Captain Smythe. The human girls will join us before first light with their things, or all of you will suffer his wrath," he says.

Jocelyn's sobs become vocal. For an instant, the pirate's face softens, but then he turns and leaves. He tramps through the now quiet dining room and out, until we no longer hear him.

Stewart goes into the dining room and returns a few moments later. "They're all gone."

That statement should ease the tossing in my stomach, but it doesn't. I won't let it show. "We should leave, too."

They all turn to face me, looking at me like I'm mad, but not daring to say a thing to a royal.

"I know there no's way off the island, but I think I know somewhere we can hide. Even if they catch us, we'll know we tried."

"She's right," Stewart says. "Gather what you need, and I'll check if they left anyone guarding the back entrance."

"Wait." Constance begins moving about the kitchen, throwing things together as she talks. "We will prepare their food first. If we have it all ready to go, they might not search as hard for the girls. Emeline, more bread. Jocelyn, go out and pick as many apples as you can. Stewart, go with Jocelyn and make sure no guards bother her, then gather any leftovers we can reuse for them from the dining room."

They jump to their tasks, Jocelyn following Stewart out the back and Emeline heading to her counter. Constance goes to work, getting the hearth going.

I slip past them, down the hall to the servants' quarters. I enter my room and shove my clothes in a bag. We have to get out of this. My plan had better come through.

Chapter
FIVE

⌒

T HE PACK ON my back feels bulky and awkward. Stewart says it is the lightest one and that he wouldn't ask me to carry it except for the fact that no one else has room. Many of our clothes got left behind. When they finished preparing the food and came to my room, Constance shook her head at the bag holding half my clothes and I let it remain on the floor. Mostly we are carrying food.

"You lead the way. I'll be right next to you in case you need anything," Stewart says. He has a few strands of gray by his thinly pointed ears, and I wonder how many more this situation will be adding to them. I used to think he was too young to have gray hairs, but now I wonder how often he deals with situations like this that cause a lot of stress.

I head out the door and through the garden. The moonlight changes it. It's even more beautiful, but in a different way. I stop to make sure everyone is following me. Stewart's right next to me, as he said he would be, followed by Emeline and Jocelyn. Constance comes last. She uses magic to cover our trail.

I try to keep a steady pace. The garden isn't the only thing that looks different in the night, and I hope I can remember my way in the dark. Every rustle has me jumping. I'm tired and heavy, but I keep pushing along. The farther we get from the castle, the more comfortable I am. The tiredness and ache are worth it. The girls chatter with each other, quietly at first, but then loudly enough so I can hear.

"It's not bad," Jocelyn says. "It's just that I want to meet someone. I know I'm still young, but I worry I won't ever find a man. Nothing is better than true love."

"Love is grand," Emeline replies.

I've never heard so much silliness.

"You know the law, though. We have to be released from her service before we can court and marry. But if that happens, we won't be able to support ourselves."

"That's enough, girls," Constance says.

They can't marry or even court? I heard about that once. Maybe I could give them some type of extra pay before they leave my service, but I'm not ready for them to leave yet. Perhaps I can amend that law when I marry. Would Prince Phillip mind? Maybe he won't want to spend time in Amara, and I'll be free to make all the choices. Or he'll want me to always be on Bardus with his humans, and I'll be able to do nothing. Like always.

Not many elves have met Prince Philip. It's been hard to get any information on him. It's not surprising since most of our contact with humans comes from trading or plundering, with the exception of the occasional human servant, like Jocelyn. It would be nice to know something other than how they only care about themselves. How they are selfish, greedy pigs. Jocelyn isn't like that, but maybe that's because she grew up with elves. Captain Smythe acted like humans are said to. What if Prince Phillip is just like him?

Worry swirls through me. I brush thoughts of it away and focus on the scenery around me. Dawn is looming, which doesn't do a thing to ease my worry. We're almost there, though. I hope the pirates won't find us in the cavern I found. The hill can be seen from over the tree tops. After another half an hour, the sun has broken through the night sky, and we stand at the base of that hill.

"This is where we're hiding?" Jocelyn asks.

"I'm sure the princess knows what she's doing," Emeline responds.

They talk more than they ever did back in Amara.

"This is almost it. I stumbled onto a cave last time I was here. The opening is hard to see."

We walk around the side of the rocky hill. A squirrel runs across the ground in front of us then scrambles up, jumping from rock to rock. The misshapen, lumpy hill hides the cave entrance so well, I'm not sure I can find it again. At one point, I backtrack.

"Are you sure this is the right place, my lady?" Stewart asks.

"No," I snap. I rub my eyes and try to use a calmer tone. "I'm pretty sure it's somewhere around here. I was touching some of the rock, exploring it, when I found the crevice. I couldn't see it after I found it."

They spread along the hill, touching it, trying to help me find the way in. I run my hand across the bumpy surface, moving it in and out. Then I move it further and further away from me. I squeeze around the dip in the hill, and the crevice sits before me.

I sag with relief. "It's here."

My servants come running. I head in first, dropping my bag to the side as soon as I'm in, and the girls follow after me. Once past the narrow opening, we come to a large cavern. The floor is fairly even, with a few rocks scattered about. The air is damp.

With a few grunts comes Stewart, followed by Constance.

"Bit of a tight fit," he says, "and it was hard to see. Hopefully that will be enough of a deterrent for the pirates."

"I've covered our tracks well enough. They won't be led straight here by our footprints, at least." Constance pulls out a few cloaks and wraps one around me. "Bit chilly. Glad we have this stuff, though. I didn't think we would need it until tonight."

She hands me a small piece of cheese and a hard roll. "Sorry it's not much," she whispers.

I eat the bread and cheese while she hands out small portions to Emeline, Jocelyn, and Stewart, and keeps some for herself. Once it's gone, I lie down. Though the ground is hard, it's easy to drift off after the night I've had.

A HAND covers my mouth. I squirm and reach for my sword. It's not there.

"Shhh. It's me," Constance whispers.

I sit up and open my eyes. Light comes in from the hole at the top of the cave, casting a weird light on everything. The others are awake, the girls sitting huddled together while Stewart stands to the side of the entrance.

"The pirates are coming," Constance says.

I nod my understanding. I tuck my knees closer to me, wrap my arms around them, and strain to hear sign of the pirates. At first I hear nothing, then the crackle of sticks and leaves being stepped on and a low murmur of voices reach the cave. I tighten my grip around my legs. *Please, please, please, don't let them find us.*

As they get closer, it feels harder to keep quiet. Their voices get louder.

"The captain wants them found now," a gruff voice shouts.

I can't help but scoot back. The farther from the voices I get, the better.

"Such a waste of time. We already got all their food, and the princess isn't here. We should get on with the job. Captain's gonna drop them in a couple weeks anyways," a second voice says.

Drop us where? What type of condition would we even be in? I use my hands to scoot back further. The sides get tighter, but my back hasn't touched the wall yet. I scoot more and bump against something. Next thing I know, a loud crash comes from behind me. My hand flies to my mouth.

"Hear that?"

"Yeah. Maybe we found them."

I hold my breath as the shuffling nears the entrance of the cave.

Chapter
SIX

〜

"NAH. IT'S NOTHING." The man's voice echoes throughout the cave. "Musta been that squirrel hopping about."

A ruckus echoes through the cave and then silence. The bread and cheese go sour inside me. Not daring to make more noise than I already have, I wrap my cloak more tightly around me and wait. I can't bring myself to meet the others' gazes.

Once in a while, we hear a scuffle outside, but it becomes so infrequent I don't know if it's the pirates lying in wait for us or an animal. Time drips by so slowly, it's hard to keep track of. I wiggle around a bit, trying to bring my limbs back to life. The cave grows dark as the sun sinks lower in the sky.

Stewart heads to the food bag and grabs a roll. "I'm going back to the castle, to check."

He shoves himself through the opening, but I can't hear him moving about after that. A few minutes of silence pass, and I gather the courage to stand and stretch. My muscles tingle. It feels so good to move. The others follow my lead, moving around a bit, but no one speaks. It feels as if there could still be a pirate coming in at any moment.

Once my body feels a bit better, I turn behind me to see what caused such a ruckus. The noise didn't sound like the scattering of rocks. In the dark, all I can see are shapes. I rub my hands together then reach down. It feels like broken pottery, but what would pottery be doing in a cave? I dig around further, careful not to get cut. My hand brushes against more pottery and then against something else. It feels heavy and rough. I grab it and hold it up toward the last remaining light.

"What have you got there?" Constance whispers.

"It looks like some type of scroll." The girls gather around me. "It was in some pottery that I knocked over." My cheeks heat, and I'm grateful for the dark, even if it means we can't read the scroll.

"Looks old," Constance says. "We'd better pack it up in something until we can handle it more delicately. Don't want to ruin it before we know what it is. Emeline, grab the bag with the blankets."

Emeline does as she's told.

"Help me wrap it in one of them. It's not the best option, but better than nothing."

Working together, Emeline and Constance wrap up the scroll and carefully place it in the bag.

"I wonder what's in it," Jocelyn says. "Do you think it's from a long time ago? No one has visited this island in so long, it has to be older than a century. Wouldn't it be fun if it was a treasure map? I've always wanted to go hunting for treasure."

"I'm sure it's nothing so silly," Constance says. She looks up at Jocelyn. "Though I suppose a treasure map would be interesting. It's probably a record of what they used to store in here, or some other household matter."

"You're right." Jocelyn sighs. "How long do you think it will be until Stewart gets back?"

Constance looks up at the hole. "Too long. Best get some more sleep or find something quiet to entertain yourselves."

WHAT FEELS LIKE several hours later, the sound of someone tromping through the woods brings me out of my daze. We stare at the entrance, though it is too dark to see anything. I hold my breath and wait, afraid it's a pirate and hoping it's Stewart. The noise moves back and forth around the entrance of the cave. I clasp my hands together to stop the trembling.

"Dagnabbit. It's me," Stewart calls. "I'm alone, but I can't find the entrance."

Jocelyn lets out a giggle, and I join in. It feels so good to laugh.

"Swear on your honor you're alone," Constance says, silencing our laughter.

"I swear."

She moves to the entrance to show him where we are.

He jams himself back through the opening and says, "They're gone. I could see their boat off in the distance when I got close to the castle. Or at least what's left of the castle. It's pretty bad."

He looks at me, but I don't know what to say. Mostly I'm happy they're gone.

"We'll deal with that when we have to," Constance says. "Would we be safer staying here or going back to the castle?"

"Probably the castle, but only because we can make it safe from animals."

They turn to me, and Stewart asks, "Is that all right, Princess?"

"Yes. Lead the way."

Constance hands me a roll to munch on while we walk, and everyone gathers the things together. I don't have a bag this time, though with the scroll tucked in one bag, I'm not sure how things fit together to make that work.

I scrunch through the opening, following Stewart out of the cave. I glance around, expecting the pirates to still be here all along and realize I've been hiding. Nothing happens.

The moon shines, lighting up our way back to the castle. My servants exit the cave, and Stewart leads us back. Everyone stays hushed, even our footsteps. Maybe they're afraid the pirates haven't really gone as well.

The events of the last couple days are unlike any I've ever lived before. It's been strange enough parading around in servants' garb, but then to have to act like a servant and take orders… Going into hiding, so pirates don't kidnap me… It feels different than slinking off on a ship to an abandoned island. It's almost exciting. Though not in any way I would want to go through again. But *pirates*. I not only survived the encounter, but it was also with the worst pirate of all.

And I did it by outsmarting him.

We enter a clearing, and several bats swoop overhead. Behind me, one of the girls lets out a small shriek. I glance around, but I can't tell if it was Emeline or Jocelyn. They both look nervous and scared. I quicken my pace, anxious to be away from the creatures. In my rush, I stumble over a branch. My crash echoes through the forest.

I sit, waiting to see if my clumsiness is going to draw out any hidden pirates. Only the hooting of an owl sounds through the trees.

"Are you all right?" Stewart puts out a hand for me to grab onto.

I stare at it. The only time I touch servants is when they are helping me dress or bathe. It's better than scrambling up by myself. I take hold of it, and he hoists me up.

"Fine, I think." I brush myself off. "Nothing a good bath and some time won't fix."

"I'll look at your scrapes when we get to some better light," Constance says.

"That would be grand."

"Let's move," Stewart says.

I follow him. We all are making more noise now. If my servant's scream and my crash didn't alert the pirates to our presence, they must truly be gone. Stewart is moving faster. I stretch my legs to keep up with him. Even in the dark of

Janeal Falor

morning, things are looking more familiar. A little bit longer, and we'll be at the castle.

Constance hands me a water skin. I stop and let the cool water trickle into my mouth. Stewart rushes on ahead. I take another pull on the water skin. Just as I move it away from my mouth, a rustling comes from somewhere nearby. Startled, I drop the water skin. Water splashes out, dampening the ground and the ends of my skirt.

I twirl around and meet the frightened gazes of my younger servants and Constance's determined one. My stomach drops. I spin back around, my wet skirt chilling my legs. My body tenses like when I'm training. I loosen my knees a bit, ready to run or fight, unsure which it will be. Should I call for Stewart, who has almost disappeared, or will that make things worse?

Before I know what to do, the rustling comes closer. I frantically look for something to use as a weapon, while holding still as can be. Before I can find anything to help, a wild boar stomps through the trees. A putrid smell assaults me. The thick brute pays no mind to me or the servants behind me. It smashes across the path, through the trees on the other side, and fades from view. I can't move for a moment, then I relax into a fit of giggles. Emeline and Jocelyn join in, and soon Constance does as well.

Stewart comes back up the path, one eyebrow raised. "Is everything all right?"

"We're fine," I manage between giggles.

He shakes his head and continues on toward the castle. He glances behind him to make sure we are coming, and I trail after him. I look over my shoulder to see Constance picking up my forgotten water skin, and then she and the girls follow.

"I've never seen such a big boar up close before that wasn't waiting to be roasted or already on a spit," Jocelyn says. "It wasn't as scary as the pirates, but it smelled about as bad. Who knew they stunk so awful?"

"I did," Emeline replies. "When I was little, my brother and I were playing in the yard when one came prancing down the street. Smelled foul. My mother came running out, afraid it was going to hurt us. Horrid creatures."

"You saw one when you were that little." Jocelyn sounds amazed. "I would have been so scared. Even more scared than I was a few minutes ago. Do you remember much else from your childhood? You've never talked much about it before. I know so little from before Constance found me. I thought maybe you were the same with your family or something."

"No. My family is still alive and healthy. Mother sent me to serving school, in hopes I'd be able to make a better life for myself."

"Amazing."

"That's what mom thou—" Emeline's voice comes to a standstill, the rest of us coming to stand beside her.

My garden is burned to ash. There is still heat rolling off it. Parts of it smolder. I blink to stave off the tears.

Stewart grimaces. "I'm sorry."

"Oh, no," Jocelyn cries.

"The whole castle is in shambles." Stewart rubs his chin. "It will take a little while, but we should be able to make a safe place to sleep inside, at least."

Constance nods. "Let's get moving then."

She herds the others inside, but I stay and stare at the ruined garden.

Chapter
SEVEN
༄

THE NEXT MORNING after a meager breakfast of biscuits, I insist we look at the scroll before going to do any work. As we open it up, I let out a soft gasp. It's more than just a list of household items. Not all of it is readable, but the part we can decipher feels like it was written for me.

There shall be an elven princess of pure heart. She will wed a human prince with a heart full of love and care.

The two will unite their people once more, and peace will again abound.

Not that I think I have a pure heart, and I can only hope the human prince I'm to marry has a heart full of love and care. But there's never been another human prince and elven princess wed before me.

What's more, if it is, could we really bring our two countries together? Could we find a peace long sought after?

I hope so. We desperately need it. What we also need is some way to make the rest of the scroll legible, if it can be done. This feels so important, as if the fate of my people rests with what it says. Maybe it's nothing, but my heart tells me it's more.

Everyone is staring at me.

I hurry to roll it back up while being as careful as possible. Once done, I carefully put it back in the sack and the others go about their chores.

It turns into a long week of putting things back together while waiting. My servants take turns watching for any ship that might dock for either help or trouble. I roam aimlessly, wondering what to do. On the seventh day in the afternoon, I give up. Since I can't work in my gardens with all the rain we've been getting, I might as well do something useful. I offer to watch the docks.

"Are you certain you can handle such a chore?" Constance asks. "It's not like working in your garden. You might as well find some handwork to do."

"No, I can do this. I don't mind."

"All right, but let's have you be lookout from inside. I don't want you catching chill."

She sets me up with a chair in the entry way with the door open and no torches on so I can't be seen if a ship does come in. Once I'm settled, she hurries away to some project or another.

I stare out at the docks. Rain drizzles on the open sea. This is just as boring, if not worse than I thought it would be. It feels good to assist them, though.

The others have been working hard, fixing things back up and acquiring food. The pirates took not only the food my servants prepared for them, but also everything else they could find. I've never been so hungry before. At least I'm not out in the rain.

Cool air brushes my cheek. I pull my cloak tighter. I tuck my legs beneath me, grab the blanket on my lap, and wrap it around me. I lean back, eyes heavy, as I stare outside. The sea is getting hard to see through the pouring.

Time passes in a creeping way that has me longing to never have asked for this chore in the first place. It's not really fitting a princess. But then, I'm not doing much to stay as a princess right now anyway. I'll just have to pretend that this never happened once I get back to Amara.

My eyelids sag. I shake my head. Someone should come to replace me soon, but not soon enough. A nap sounds lovely. I'll take one before dinner. Or rather, before my evening snack. A yawn escapes my lips, and I fight to remain alert. This is important; I can't fail. I think of the bed awaiting me. Its horror of a mattress is usually enough to keep me awake, but now I'd sleep in it despite the hard lumps. Closing my eyes, I imagine slipping into my bed at home. The silk sheets and the soft mattress cradling me. My body feels so heavy.

Figures are a blur on both sides of me. My feet brush against grass and rose petals. I watch my step through a sheer white veil. My heart is pounding and my mouth is dry as I reach the end of the aisle. Nausea twists through my stomach when I see the two shoes waiting for me. My throat constricts as someone lifts the veil off my face. I follow the movement with my gaze and see a man dressed in fashionable, formal attire. The sick feeling increases.

My heart pounds harder while I struggle to keep myself bolted to the spot. The man's unfamiliar face comes into view.

"Phillip?" I whisper.

The man distorts, his face twisting until it becomes that of Captain Smythe.

I scream.

I jolt awake, and my blanket falls to the floor. The cold shocks me fully conscious. The thought of marrying Captain Smythe makes me ill, but I don't know that Prince Phillip is any better. He could be worse. Hot tears fill my eyes, and I wipe them away.

A breeze sweeps through the front door, raising goosebumps on my arms. Guilt fills me when I realize I haven't been paying attention. I scan the sea. The rain has slowed to a drizzle. This will be a nice change.

Then I see a ship heading for our island.

I jerk out of the chair and rush to the kitchen. Constance looks up from her soup when I come in.

"There's a ship almost to the docks," I say. "The flags are all down, so I don't know what color they are. I couldn't see any identifying marks."

"Go to your room. I'll warn the others. Get your disguise ready, in case anyone comes."

Feeling sick, I nod, but Constance has already hurried off. I stand in the empty kitchen. When no one comes back screaming about pirates, I head to my room. It wasn't much before, but it's worse now. I don't bother to close the door. Stewart tried to fix it, but it still doesn't like to close tight. He's out hunting now. I could be taken or dead before he knows there's anyone on the island.

I pace the room, trying to rid myself of such morbid thoughts. We survived once; we can do it again. A low fire crackles in the fireplace. For several long minutes, it's all I hear. The warmth of the blaze helps chase the goosebumps away.

It was a large ship, so I doubt it's someone coming to pick us up early. Unless my parents somehow got news of my trouble and sent a whole troop to guard me on the way home. With no identifying marks, it's not likely. It could be the very people threatening my life. Footsteps tread down the hall. I halt, shaking. Before the person reaches my room, I remember I still look like me. With a stab of pain, I change my face, eyes, ears, and hair.

The footsteps are almost here. My mouth is dry.

Emeline comes into view, and the tension inside me unravels.

"It's a group of merchants who had some troubles in the storm, Princess. Constance is down on the dock, talking to them. She requested that you remain disguised, as a precaution."

"Isn't this a little far out for merchants to be?"

"I wouldn't know, ma'am. Human traders don't interest me."

"They're human?"

She nods. *Humans.* A bunch together, and up close. More than I've ever been around at one time, I would guess. At least, not counting the pirates, which I certainly do not.

A nervous yet excited fluttering dances through me. "I will be down at the docks, Emeline."

She widens her eyes then lowers her head. "Yes, ma'am."

I scurry past her. While hurrying down the hall, I pull the hood of my cloak up over my head. It doesn't keep water out as well as I'm used to, but it's better than nothing. I open the front door. The drizzle has picked back up to a steady rain. I hesitate, but I don't know when I'll get this chance again. The fresh scent is invigorating. I head out, careful not to step in the puddles as I stroll to the dock.

Constance stands on the beach. I stand next to her, my clothes getting damp.

She turns to me and narrows her eyes. "You should stay out of sight," she whispers, the boat right next to us.

Before I can respond, a conversation on the boat catches my attention. I can't see who's speaking, but their words drift to us over the pattering rain.

"Can't believe we had to stop at a place with elves. See 'em too much as it is, with the tradin' and all. If it weren't for this blasted storm, we could have been almost to Amara by now. Instead, we're stuck with 'em longer. I'd find a new job if this one didn't pay so well."

"Hear, hear. I'd rather show them how we feel than pretending to play nice through trade. Can't even jack up our prices on them," a second voice replies.

"Can't imagine what the king and queen were thinking, tying us to 'em through marriage. Hope that princess of theirs knows what's good for her and stays in the elven castle."

"Hush up now."

After a few seconds of silence, a third voice says, "Go help with the mast while the captain talks with them."

I twist my hands within the folds of my skirt. I hear nothing else from them, but what I did hear makes me feel I should have stayed in the castle. The more I learn about humans, the more I wonder if the people trying to take my life are right. They shouldn't be trying to kill me to accomplish their goal; they only need to let me spend some time with these horrid humans.

I don't know if I should go or stay and discover more about the humans, but the decision is made for me as three sailors head down the gangplank. They tread their way across the dock and over to us. The first one looks like he must be the captain. A second one stands over to his side. He's about my age, with blonde hair and mousy brown eyes. The third one stops next to the captain, right in front of me.

I can't take my eyes off him.

My head comes to his chin. His sandy hair is cut short, and his golden eyes hold a certain warmth. Something unfamiliar stirs within my chest. My mouth goes dry as he looks me in the eye. I refocus my gaze on their older leader, but the sailor holds my attention.

"I've heard you have had some problems. I'm Captain Zaccheus. This is Abner, and this is Robert." The captain points to them as he says their names. Robert is the one I'm intrigued with.

"I'm Constance. Captain Smythe attacked our island, leaving us with no food. Our boat isn't supposed to be back for a while. We would be willing to trade labor for food."

"Captain Smythe, you say? Was anyone injured?"

I shudder as she responds. "No. We were lucky. Our things were not so fortunate. We've been making do, but they burned the garden, making food harder to come by."

"Robert, go round up a box of food for them."

Robert heads back for the ship, and I feel a little more at ease as the captain continues. "Do you need help planting or repairing anything as well?"

"No, thank you," Constance says. "We're on leave, and not really used to having such idle hands. Fixing a few things up is no problem."

"Maybe you can be of help to us, then. The storm caught us by surprise. It was a nasty one. We're supposed to be in Amara in three days, but we're falling behind. We need to make some repairs as quickly as possible. A few supplies, and some extra help would go a long way to assisting us reach our destination as soon as possible."

"Of course. There's an elf with us who would know how to help. The rest of us will do what we can as well. Maybe we could use the labor as payment for food."

"I think that would work." Captain Zaccheus turns to Robert as he rejoins us, and so do I. "Robert, would you be so kind as to take that food to where they want it while I finish making some arrangements? This servant girl here can show you the way."

"Certainly." Those golden eyes turn to me. I stare back at them in a daze. Robert says, "If that's all right with you, miss?"

I raise my brows in confusion, then realize I'm the servant girl mentioned. I don't know if I can ever get used to that—following someone else's orders doesn't sit well—but I do want to spend a little more time with Robert. See what draws me to him, and maybe get more of an insight into humans. Captain Zaccheus is more like Jocelyn than the others. I hope Robert is too, though it's probably a fluke.

"I can go if you would like, Robert." Abner moves as if to come with us. He is a bit taller than me, but the scowl on his face is intimidating.

"I have this, all right. If the lady doesn't mind."

"By all means." I don't mind being with him at all. That Abner character, on the other hand, makes me uncomfortable. "Follow me," I say to Robert.

Abner sneers at me and heads back to the ship. Not a comfortable gesture, to be sure, but better than Constance's glower as I leave. I'm going back to the castle like she wanted, so I don't think she has reason to be displeased.

Robert and I start up the path.

"I fear I didn't catch your name," he says when we're almost there.

"Adelei."

"Pleasure to meet you."

My palms grow damp with sweat as I open the castle door. I lead him through the halls to the kitchen and point at the table. "You can leave it there."

He puts the box on the table and turns his large frame toward me. I struggle to find something to say. Nothing comes to mind. How can nothing come to me? I turn, hoping there's an object in the room to talk about. Instead, I stumble over a chair and fly toward the floor.

The world rushes past. Suddenly, it stops. Two hands are secure around my waist before I crash to the ground. He pulls me up, his chest brushing my back.

"Are you unharmed?" he asked.

A startling heat fills my face. "No. Yes. I mean, yes, I'm not hurt. Thank you."

"You're welcome." His hands slip off my waist.

I reluctantly pull away and pick up a piece of the broken chair I tripped over. "Captain Smythe's handiwork. Or maybe one of his crew. I thought the others had all of them put back together. Guess I haven't been paying enough attention."

"Heard stories about him. Glad you were able to come through the encounter unharmed." My heart beats faster. He holds out his hand for the broken pieces. "I could probably fix that. Doesn't look too difficult."

I hand the pieces to him, wishing they were small enough for our hands to touch. What's wrong with me? I don't know this common, human sailor. He's kind, though. Kinder than I expected. "That would be helpful. If you don't need to get back to your ship right away, that is," I say.

"It's not a problem. I'm not really skilled at the things they need fixed up. But hammering a few nails in a chair I can handle."

"Nails?" I glance down at my fingernails, wondering what he would need those for. Though mine are worked on daily back home, I never realized they could help with fixing up a chair. Then I remember he's talking about a tool carpenters and others sometimes use. "Right. Nails. I'm not sure we have any or where they'd be."

He stares at me, brows crinkled. His lips turn up in a smile that makes me feel weak. "I'm sure we can locate some," he says.

He sets the pieces on the table next to the box of food. It groans and creaks. With a snap, the legs of the table give out. Robert reaches for the box of food. It looks like his fingers have the side of it, but then it goes crashing to the floor.

Chapter
EIGHT

ൟ

ROBERT LOOKS at me, eyes wide. "I can fix that, too."
I can't help but laugh, and his tense face relaxes.
"Don't worry over it," I say. "Fits in with everything
else around here."

He leans over and puts the food box to the side. "At least
it landed upright and didn't spill much. Your food may be a
bit jostled, though."

"Food is food, even if it's jostled."

He grins up at me, and warmth fills me. Hovering over
the mess, he shifts through the broken pieces. "Hold this for
me, please." He holds out some pieces of wood, and I take
them from him.

As he works, his muscles flex beneath his shirt. Realizing
I'm staring, I avert my gaze to the hearth. I cradle the scraps
close to me.

"It will need a leg replaced, but the rest of it doesn't look so bad." He stands a few inches from me.

I'm conscious of his proximity. His warmth. His smell—a salty musky scent that lingers in a comforting way. Without looking, I know he's watching me. I hold the scraps out toward him, and his arms brush against mine as he helps me hold the pile.

We touch. As if in a trance, I turn and look at him. Tingles run up my arms where his skin meets mine, almost like magic but more intense. The current passing between us is so powerful I can't release the scraps to him or look away.

We lean toward one another. Closer. His breath is warm on my cheek. His eyes hold an emotion I don't recognize but feel within myself. At the same time he tilts his head down to me, I raise my head toward him.

The kitchen door opens so hard it bangs against the wall.

We spring apart, and the scraps fall back to the floor between us. The room seems dark and colder. I sneak a quick peek at Robert. His face glows, lighting the space around him. I look at the stone floor, and heat rises to my cheeks as the strange warm feeling stirs within me.

Emeline rushes into the room. "What was that? What happened, Prin—um, Adelei?"

"Your table couldn't hold everything I put on it." Robert runs his hand through his hair. "I can fix it, though. I think. Let me go get some tools."

He rushes out of the room.

"Are you all right?" Emeline asks me.

"Yes, I'm fine." I don't feel fine. I feel different. Warm and tingly. My pulse is still racing.

"Well, then, let me see about putting something together to eat."

She grabs the box of food, sets it on the counter, and starts looking through it.

"Sounds fantastic," I say. "I'm going to go lie down for a while. Let me know when it's ready or if I need to pretend to do some chores because one of the humans comes back around."

"Yes, ma'am."

I head to my room in a bit of a daze. Part of me wants to stay in the kitchen for when Robert gets back, but part of me is frightened to. My thoughts turn to being near him. His face inches from mine. His arms against mine. I'm not sure what to think, but I like it. I cross the room and lie on my bed.

I can't afford to like it.

I STARE OUT the open kitchen door, at the rain drizzling on my scorched garden. Emeline, Jocelyn, and Constance are cooking behind me. Robert and another sailor fixed the table hours ago and went back to their ship. Stewart followed them down to see what he could do to help on the ship. I vacillate between wishing he had a reason to come back and hoping I don't see him again.

I shouldn't have looked out at the garden. Jocelyn's bubbly chatter was lifting my spirits until I did. With a sigh, I turn my back on the ruins. I sit at the table in front of a bowl of fruit and pick up the knife lying next to it, to toy with. Everyone is so busy. I hate to interrupt them for a piece of fruit.

With my free hand, I grab a mango. I stare at it. I bring the knife to the fruit and push it in. Waving the knife, now hidden with the fruit, it reminds me of some of the council members that do nothing but bob their heads up and down. I put the fruit back in my hand and drive down the knife.

It slices into my palm. "*Ow.*"

Constance rushes over. "What happened?" She puts the fruit on the table and looks at my hand. "Jocelyn, run and grab some bandages. Emeline, get some clean water, please."

The girls rush to their tasks.

"I was just trying to cut a mango to eat," I say.

Constance tsks. Emeline sits a bowl of water and a rag on the table.

"Thank you. That is all," Constance says.

Emeline moves back to the counter. "Yes, ma'am."

Constance dips the rag in the water and then gently presses it to my cut. "I'd have thought with all your fencing, you would have known better than to cut something in your hand like that."

"You do it all the time."

"I've had more practice than you." She dabs at the cut, which has stopped bleeding. "It isn't deep. You'll be fine if we keep it clean. Try not to move your hand too much so the healing process can happen."

Jocelyn rushes out of the hall with an armful of bandages. "I've got them."

"Those will certainly be enough to take care of this little wound," Constance says.

Jocelyn's face turns red. "I didn't know how bad it was. I'll put the extras away when we're done."

"Hold this while I tie it."

Jocelyn holds the bandage in place, while Constance knots it together. It pinches a bit, and then feels normal. Once it's finished, Constance inspects it. "Thank you, Jocelyn. After you put the bandages away, will you check on the soup for me?"

"I'd be happy to. It may take me a minute, though. I made a bit of a mess in my hurrying about."

Constance nods. "Soup will be there when you're done."

"Yes, ma'am." Jocelyn scurries out with her arms full of linen scraps.

I pull at the loose ends of my bandage as the work continues on around me.

Stewart strides in the room. "My lady, would you please join me and Constance?"

"I would." I stand and follow him down the hall to Constance's room.

We enter the room, and I take the only chair. Constance sits on the bed, and Stewart stands by the door.

"We're lucky that this is a merchant ship and not something worse," Stewart says. "One close encounter with pirates is more than I wanted."

Constance scoffs. "It wasn't so bad."

"Only because something was holding them back at first, and we weren't here when they finally let loose," Stewart says.

Constance's eyes tighten, but before she can respond, Stewart continues. "There was something odd about them. That's what I wanted to discuss. I understand the king's plan, but I fear your location was leaked, my lady. More danger is probably already on its way."

"I agree," Constance says. "They seemed sure she was here."

He nods. "I don't how it happened, but I'd feel better if we left with this merchant ship. Your parents won't know where you are, but then neither will any spies."

"You think there are spies in my parents' court?" I can't imagine someone turning on my family.

"Unfortunately, it's a real possibility. We'll worry about discovering the traitor or traitors once we have you well guarded. If we hitch a ride, we should be able to make it all the way to Amara within a week or two."

He's right that I'm not safe here, but is going with strange humans any better? Maybe not, but it's better than waiting around. Plus I'll get a chance to see what humans are like up close. "Your advice is sound. We should make travel arrangements with them."

"I agree," Constance says. "Do they have room for all of us?"

"Yes. I learned that half of their goods were damaged in the storm. Worst comes to it, we could sleep with the cargo." He looks at me. "It won't be comfortable."

"Neither was the journey here. I'll live."

He nods and turns to leave.

"Wait, I just had a thought." Constance scrutinizes me before continuing. "There's a problem. We haven't yet figured out the consequences of this spell you will be continually performing. If we undertake this journey, you need to use it much more than I'm comfortable with, given how little we know."

"She's right," Stewart says. "We don't know what harm it may be causing."

After a couple minutes, the spell becomes a background thought. After a few hours, it becomes as much a part of me as breathing. The reminder it could be doing me harm sets me on edge.

I brush imaginary crumbs from my dress. "What other option do I have? My parents won't know something is wrong, so they won't send a ship to pick us up early. Will any other ship even come? If it does, it's likely to have the same predicament, with me having to disguise myself. Except they may not be people we trust to sail with."

Constance stands and puts a hand on my shoulder. "We don't have any other good options, but I want to make sure you're aware that we don't know what risk this carries for you. Are you all right with having to deal with the unintended consequences?"

"I'll have to be. Let us hope whatever the consequences end up being, they're something we can deal with."

Chapter
NINE

❧

THE MERCHANT SHIP looms over me as I follow Stewart up the gangplank. I try to make myself as servant-like as possible—the condition on which I was able to accompany him to talk to Captain Zaccheus. That and keeping by Stewart while not saying anything. I didn't agree to keep quiet. If there's something I want to say, I'm going to say it, but I said I'd stay by Stewart. I'm not completely daft.

As we make our way on deck, a couple of crew members skirt around us.

"Pardon me," Stewart calls out. The two men stop and turn toward us, and he asks, "Where can I locate Captain Zaccheus?"

Both men stay silent, shifting their weight as they eye Stewart, paying particular attention to his ears. At least mine look human at the moment. That may be a point in our favor.

"The helm," one says, hands balling into fists.

"Thank you," Stewart replies, but the men run off before the words are out of his mouth. *Completely uncivilized. Though there are times I wish I could get away with such behavior.*

Stewart sighs and turns toward the helm. "Let's get this over with."

We walk across the tidy deck and stop several feet away from the captain and a crew member he's speaking with. Captain Zaccheus isn't as huge as Captain Smythe, but he still towers over those around him. I can't tell how old he is just by looking at him. His skin is darkened from the sun and a bit wrinkly, but his hazel eyes twinkle with youth. The short cut of his hair makes it harder to see its slate color, though there are still specks of black in it.

The crew member he's conversing with holds himself at attention with a manner of respect. The captain points at the younger man and says something I can't hear. The man nods and leaves, not bothering to glance at us. Captain Zaccheus turns to us with a smile. I smile back, grateful there's another person who won't treat us coldly on this ship, besides Robert.

"Can we have a word with you?" Stewart asks.

"Go ahead. I'm free," the captain replies.

"We have a favor to ask. After the pirates took or destroyed most of our things, we're not prepared to wait for the ship that's supposed to come back for us. We were wondering if you'd give us passage on your ship, even if we need to sleep in the cargo hold, in exchange for our labor and cooking. Constance is the best cook you'll ever find."

"We'd be happy to have you. No need to sleep in the cargo hold, though. We've room to spare. Passengers travel with us sometimes, used to more often. Be good to have someone about. Also, no need to worry about labor. You already helped us repair the ship."

"Constance would be put off if she couldn't at least cook for you," Stewart replies. No doubt he will be helping as much as they'll let him, as well. I smile as he continues. "When are you setting sail?"

"Tomorrow. The storm has already set us behind. I'm hoping to get to Amara as soon as possible with our supplies. Fortunately, we don't have to head back to Bardus right away, so there is some leeway."

While they continue to work out details, I wander over the side of the ship and rest my hands on the railing. When will I head to Bardus, the human country? I don't know. It's never been discussed around me.

"I don't think so." Robert's voice pulls me from my musings. I glance around but don't see him, though he sounds close by. "I'm not ready to settle down anyway, Abner."

"My sister is an excellent match for you." Abner's voice is different now that it doesn't have a sneering undertone. I wouldn't have known it was his if Robert didn't call him by name.

"She's excellent, but you know how things are. Can we please discuss something else?"

"Gladly. I bet I can win you now. I've been practicing."

Robert chuckles. "You haven't beaten me since we were leaving little foot prints all over the gardens. Are you confident you have improved enough?"

"I see how it is. You're afraid I'll beat you."

Robert's laugh comes harder, but before I hear his response, Stewart taps me on the shoulder.

"We're good for tomorrow. We'll be home before you know it. And hopefully no worse than when we left," he says.

One can hope. "Thank you, Stewart."

He waves me back toward the gangplank. I head toward it but stop when I find Robert and Abner in front of me. Robert's facing me, but his golden-eyed gaze is focused on Abner, who has his back to me.

"You should take better care of your sword," Robert says.

"It's not my fault. You know it's not. Old Ben usually—" He stops and turns when Robert elbows him, and they both look at us. Abner's face is relaxed, except for a few smile lines around his small mouth. For a moment, he almost looks friendly. As soon as he sees us, his face hardens, and he appears to be a different person.

Robert's the only kind one now. He looks like he could charm Constance out of making him work. But Abner's scowl is enough to scare mother out of her petticoats. Or burst me into flames.

Stewart takes hold of my elbow. He wants me to go around and quickly be away, but my feet carry me closer to the humans. I focus on Rober and keep heading that way. He looks so much like an elf, except for those oddly rounded ears. His skin hasn't been darkened from the sun like the others on the boat—though neither has Abner's.

There's something different about Robert. Something that draws me forward.

"Adelei, Stewart, what brings you aboard?" Robert asks.

"We discussed traveling with you, when you leave for Amara, with the captain." Stewart speaks before I know what to say.

"Did he consent?"

"He did."

Robert nods as if he expected nothing else. "We're leaving soon. Is there any way I can assist your prepare?"

Abner shifts his glare to Robert.

Stewart hesitates before replying. "If you don't mind, there are a few larger items I could use help carrying."

"Certainly. Abner here was just about to see what he could do about cleaning up his sword."

"If you'll excuse me, Robert," Abner says through his teeth and stomps away, taking the tension in the air with him.

"Shall we?" Robert scoots to the side to let me pass first.

I skirt ahead of them, my steps light on the deck. Stewart falls in behind me with Robert at his side.

We arrive at the castle. I hesitate at the door before I remember I'm a servant and must open it myself. Robert's so engrossed in conversation with Stewart, I hope he didn't notice my error. Once in the hall, I step aside, unsure of where Stewart's planning on taking him. I contemplate heading to my room, but it's droll there.

Stewart is talking as they walk in, so he doesn't glance my way, but Robert briefly catches my eyes. Heat creeps across my cheeks. Thankfully, he's already passed by so he couldn't have seen. The lower class is not usually so direct with me, especially those who do not work with me often.

I run my hands over my coarse dress, trying to smooth it out as we enter the kitchen. It's empty of servants, but the fire still burns, so I place myself to the side of it where I can see the whole room.

Stewart glances from me to the servants' enterance, to Robert, and back again.

"I need to see how Constance is coming along with the packing." Stewart's gaze bores into me.

I think he needs to make sure there's nothing out that Robert shouldn't see. Taking his hint, I say, "I can keep Robert company while you do so." I'm not sure I want to. It's nice to have the opportunity to learn more about humans, but I don't feel comfortable with him by myself. There's been enough one-on-one time with him.

An awkward tension thickens the room.

"Please take a seat, Robert," I say. "The chairs should hold your weight now."

"I'm willing to put that to the test. Thank you." He pulls back one of the chairs and hovers on it. After a few seconds, he relaxes into it.

"I'll be right back, then." Stewart's jaw tightens before he leaves down the hall. What could be bothering him?

His departure is followed by silence. And more silence. My lack of manners would be appalling at court. It's easier to make conversation there, though. What do humans speak of?

I shift my weight around so my back is toward the fire. "You're a sailor." Profound I am not.

"Yes. And you are a servant." He runs his fingers through his hair and gives me a warm smile.

"For the princess, you know." Court would be tearing me to pieces. Human court had better be easier to converse in than this, or I'll be a mocked fool the rest of my life.

"Indeed? I wasn't aware of that. Are you enjoying the break?"

He has no idea. How do I answer that? I'm not sure I know the answer. "It's different. Nice in its way. Except the pirates, of course. The island is interesting."

"I haven't seen much of it, but it appears quite beautiful. If we had time, I wouldn't mind seeing more of it. Schedules, though. More time at sea than on land."

"You enjoy sailing, then?

He eases back further in his chair and puts his hands behind his head. "I do. There's something freeing about it. Something about being in the fresh sea air, being on a boat with only water to be seen. It's another world."

"I've never thought much about it, but I suppose the sea is a world of its own. I guess I need to stop and pay attention next time I'm sailing."

"This week you can give it a chance. Do you travel by boat much, working for the princess?"

"On occasion, I get to. Perhaps once or twice a year." I realize I'm twisting my hand within the folds of my skirt, and I force it still while working to find a safer topic. "What about your friend? Abner? Do you travel together often? Have you known each other long?"

Robert grins, and I relax with the safe topic choice. "I can't remember a time without Abner," he says. "He's been a friend my whole life. Don't know where I would be without him. He's always looking out for me."

I frown. This must be the side of Abner I caught a glimpse of on the boat. I walk to the table and sit across from Robert. "It must be splendid to have such a friend."

"There's no one like Abner. He's good at keeping an eye out for me," Robert chuckles. "Though he really can't seem to keep his sword in good condition."

"I bet I could show him a thing or two."

Robert raises his brows. "Really?"

My cheeks heat at my bold statement. "Yes, well, I've used a sword most of my life. My teacher would never allow me to treat any sword ill."

"Good for your teacher." He pauses, an inquisitive look in his eye. "If it's not too impertinent of me to ask, how did you come to have such a teacher? I don't mean to pry, but I didn't know they'd teach a servant to the princess such a skill. You've made me curious."

I open and close my mouth several times. What can I say to that? He's correct. There's little chance one of my servants would have a fencing master. Truth of the matter is the opportunity wouldn't ever be considered. "I don't know. I suppose I'm lucky."

"You don't know?" He leans closer and rests his arms on the table, hands clasped together.

"Found them." Stewart saunters into the kitchen but stops short as he looks at us. I want to hug him for interrupting.

Constance strides in behind him.

"Excellent. Are you ready for me, then?" Robert asks.

"Yes, please. If you would follow me."

I stand when Constance stops me.

"Adelei, I need your help."

Avoiding her sharp gaze, I say, "Yes, ma'am. It's been a pleasure speaking with you, Robert."

Before he can reply, Constance whisks me from the room. Clearly, she's spent too much time assisting me and not enough time in court.

"That was impolite," I say, once we are out of hearing from the kitchen.

"It's not my manners I'm worried about. Stewart shouldn't have left you alone with that man. He tried to hint as much to you, but you went ahead and stayed with him anyway."

"I thought he wanted me to keep him company. Entertain him while he found you. That has always been one of my duties."

Constance shakes her head. "Entertaining isn't the job of a servant. Even if we did want someone to entertain him, it doesn't change who you are. Please keep your distance from the sailors, especially if the rest of us aren't around."

"He doesn't seem like the type to do harm, and it's not like my reputation can be damaged under these circumstances."

"That's beside the point. While we're aboard their ship, I would prefer it if you avoided speaking to any of the crew without me or Stewart present."

Mentally, I let out a groan. Once I got talking to Robert, it wasn't so bad. Oh, well. There would probably be more awkwardness than I wish to deal with. "Yes, ma'am."

Chapter
TEN

❧

I PACE THREE STEPS across the cabin before I have to turn. My leg bumps against the narrow bunk. If it wasn't so unladylike, I'd kick it. The diminutive dresser, crammed between my bunk and an identical one for Constance, holds a few clothes for us both. All we have left.

At least I'm short enough I don't have to stoop under the low ceiling. I force myself to sit on the miniature bed and hesitantly put my weight on it. Even after several days on the ship, it's hard to trust that the bed will really hold me.

The wooden walls are caving in on me, stifling every breath. It needs a window. Without one, it feels even tighter and closed in, like a prison. No one's here. There's no reason for me to keep standing on ceremony when frustration crawls all over me. I fling myself back onto the bed, only to sit up again.

Never thought I'd have a bed worse than the one back on Sulamay Island, but I was wrong. I lower myself back onto it, trying to ignore the random pieces of straw poking my backside. If they knew who I was, maybe things would be better. Of course Jocelyn's and Emeline's bunks hold the same uncomfortable circumstances.

The air in the cabin is musty and dank. My stomach twists and churns with the rocking of the boat. I wish the journey wouldn't take so long. The captain expects the trip to take ten days—if the weather stays pleasant. Right now, it might as well be a year.

At least I'm not as sea sick as I was the first couple of days, but somehow it makes the days pass more slowly. If only Constance wasn't so insistent I stay in here while the rest of them do work around the boat. Apparently, Adelei is only skilled at helping the princess.

The four days melt together. Constance gave me some stitching, which I ignore. What's the point? Besides, on this boat, I'm likely to poke myself in the finger. The days are sweltering, leaving my servants' garb sticking to me. I long to return to Sulamay Island. The island had already begun to feel more like home than Amara. If only I could be back in my cool garden before the pirates burned it.

The only other thing that crosses my mind is Robert. Something about him makes me want to draw nearer. Though I haven't seen him since boarding the ship, my thoughts linger on him. On that brief touch. Why would I have such a connection to a human? What's more: what exactly does it mean?

It doesn't matter. I am betrothed. That's all my future contains. My parents were wrong to sell my heart so they could have a treaty, even if it is my duty. If it wasn't so utterly abhorrent to break a betrothal, I'd plead to have it done.

Especially after meeting Robert. Funny that not long ago the idea of following my heart was silly. But here I am.

Before mine, there wasn't a betrothal in my kingdom for centuries. Yet, they chose me for it. *Me.* Not that I'd have married for love, but I'd appreciate a little more say in the matter. There's no hope now, though. Nothing can stop it.

Except maybe my death.

That's it. I refuse to stay in this room a moment longer. The ache inside me is too much to stay locked in here. I feel the stabbing of changing myself to Adelei and burst out of my room and up the stairs.

The breeze sweeps across my skin, cooling me with its salty scent. The sun shines bright on the clean deck. A few crew members move about, ignoring me. Just as well; I don't want their attention.

I hurry toward the ship's railing, intent on staring out over the ocean as long as such freedom is left to me. However long it is won't be enough.

Before I can reach the railing, Abner steps in front of me, halting my progress. His gaze is tortuous, making me want to step away. Mother's training won't permit such a thing, though. Royalty never gives in unless they want to.

His mousy eyes fill with disgust, giving life to the otherwise dull brown. Dirty blond hair moves devilishly in the wind, while his frame stands tense. Though he's thin and wiry, he's still bigger than me and could do some damage if he tried.

"What do we have here?" He sneers. "All of you *servants* are supposed to be slaving away in the kitchen. You think you are better than everyone else?"

"I fear I don't have any skills in the kitchen. I ju—"

"You're as bad as those elves trying to get a free ride." He lowers his voice to a whisper as sinister as his eyes have grown. "I know what elves do with magic. If I see any of your friends doing magic on this ship..." He leans closer and pounds his fist into the flat of his hand several times before walking off.

My knees buckle. I force myself to walk the rest of the distance to the railing where I collapse against it. The salty air clears my mind of his behavior so I can focus on the threat. If I warned Stewart and Constance against using magic, it should be enough. I hope it is.

There's movement to my side, and I worry he's coming back to harm me. I reach for my sword, only to remember that they insisted I wouldn't need it on this journey. Fine. A fist works just as well if it comes to that. I turn, ready to defend myself if needed.

"Whoa, it's me." Robert holds up his hands. "Who did you expect you'd need to protect yourself from on this ship? There's only us, and the captain promised we'd take good care of you."

I shake myself. I want to tell him, but Abner is his friend. "No one, I suppose. I think I'm still uneasy after Captain Smythe's attack."

His expression grows serious as he contemplates my words. "I'm sorry you had to go through that. People like him should be locked up with the key thrown into the depths of the ocean."

I smile. "That I can agree to."

Neither of us says anything else, and things turn awkward. I twist my hands within the folds of my skirt and glance everywhere but at Robert. The wind picks up, and the waves crash on the side of the ship, filling the silence with the waves' rhythmic motions.

Robert shuffles his feet. "How has the boat ride been for you, so far?"

"Fine." Not at all the truth. "Boring, actually. I don't have experience that's useful on a ship, so I'm finding myself with nothing to do."

"That would make the journey tedious. I haven't seen you out on deck. Staying in your cabin will make the journey worse. You should come out and enjoy the fresh air."

"Yes, well…" I shrug, not looking at him.

"I can leave if that is what you'd like. I don't mean to make you uncomfortable." He takes a step away.

"No. Please, don't leave. I enjoy your company." I still my hand. "I'm sorry for my sharp tone. It is just that I—I enjoy your company, as a friend. I didn't mean to give you the wrong impression."

After a moment of hesitation, he steps forward, and a smile slips back on his face. "I enjoy your company as well."

I sneak glances at him, which would embarrass me, but he seems to be doing the same. I can't help but think of the time our hands touched. The heat rising to my cheeks.

That won't do.

I hurry to break the silence. "Would you tell me about yourself?"

"What do you want to know?"

Everything. Did I just think that? "What about your family? What are they like?"

"Well, um… As I grew up, we traveled frequently. We have a circle of friends that we converse with a lot, but other than that, we mostly keep to ourselves."

"That's all? Do you have any siblings? They'd make traveling more interesting."

"No. I am an only child."

"What did you do while traveling, then? And where did you travel to?"

He runs his hand through his sandy hair. "A few places. Around. Fabrica and Derelinquo Fork. I've been through Leviden Forest many times, and my father and I hiked up Mount Indicium once."

Safe subject. "I'm afraid I haven't heard of any of those places."

"Really?" His forehead wrinkles. "They're all on Bardus. I thought you'd know about your own land."

This is what I get for not paying attention to foreign affairs. What a fool I am. "I suppose I've spent too much time in Amara with the elves."

He nods. "Have you heard of the Crimson Ruins?"

"Now *that* one I have heard of. The abandoned isle. Not too far from Sulamay, yes?"

"Yup. Since no one has been banished there for years, Captain Zaccheus gained permission to harvest fruit from it. The mangos there grow like weeds and are the most delicious

I've ever tasted. He turns quite a profit for them in Amara. In any case, that is where we left before the storm hit, and it's somewhere we've traveled that you've heard of."

"Mangos? They're my favorite. I will have to try one from there some time."

"It's too bad we lost most of them in the storm, or I'd bring you one." He runs his finger through his hair again. "Tell me about yourself, Adelei. It's not often you see a human working for elves."

Several crew members scrubbing the deck clean pass us by. Lying to pirates is one thing. Lying to him is something else entirely, but necessary. "I was an orphan, wandering from place to place, when young Princess Arabella's ship docked on my island. Constance saw me, and I suppose she took pity on me. She took me with her and over time taught me how to be a servant for the princess."

"You must feel a great deal for Constance. Your voice sounds respectful when you speak of her."

"She's like a mother to me." I can't help but smile at that truth.

"What about Princess Arabella? Do you find her to be kind?"

Describing one's self is rather awkward. "I think she is. I know some would disagree. Many who see her say she's exceptionally beautiful, but I believe most elves are."

Robert's voice is so faint, I have to lean in closer to hear him over the waves. "If she looks anything like you, she must be beautiful," he says.

"She looks nothing like me." I pull away and stare ahead at the ocean. "Her hair is brown, and her eyes are blue as this ocean, and that's the start of it. We look nothing alike."

"I didn't mean to offend you. It's just that, in all my travels, I've never met a human as fair as you."

"You still have much traveling to do." I cringe realizing that wasn't only a rude thing to say, but also a stupid one. It wasn't that long ago he told me all the places he has been. At this rate, I'm going to do nothing but draw more attention to myself and hurt him while doing so.

He peers down at me, eyes clouded with confusion. "I suppose so."

"I am sor—" The words get stuck in my throat as I spot a dark speck tainting the fog. I search harder, hoping the second glance will pierce through the mist and tell me the boat with black sails was just my imagination.

"Adelei, are you all right?"

Without tearing my gaze from the boat, I say, "I think there's a boat with black sails coming toward us."

I sense his body tense as he grasps the rail next to me, knuckles turning white. As time ticks away, his hands regain their color. "I don't see anything. Perhaps you saw a bird? Besides, the lookout would have seen it by now."

"Would you please get a telescope and check for me? Maybe they missed something." Which they definitely have. The ship is still far, far off, but getting closer.

"Yes, my lady. Let me round one up."

Cold stabs up my spine as I wait for him to return. The boat is clear now. Sharp elven eyes, even ones disguised as a human's spot the familiar sails. Captain Smythe is headed straight toward us.

No plan of action is forthcoming. Where can we run when we're already out on the ocean? I will be captured, along with the ship and taken away whether I appear human or not.

"Found one." Robert rejoins me. "Let's take a look."

He puts the telescope to his eye. His face pales, and he lets out a curse.

Chapter
ELEVEN

E SNAPS THE telescope shut and whirls toward the crew. "Pirates."

Everyone stops what they're doing, expressions hardening. Captain Zaccheus hustles over to us, grabs the offered telescope and looks in the direction of the pirate ship. Only a brief moment later, he says, "Looks like they're headed this way, and they're coming fast. Do we stand and fight or try to outrun them?"

Robert runs his hand across the newly grown stubble on his chin. "Best to stay out of confrontation at this point. Aren't we close to Port Varas? Maybe it would be best to make it there and stop for the time being."

"Yes, Port Varas isn't far." The captain turns to yell at the crew. "Make course forty-six degrees."

Men scramble about in different directions. I hope it's enough. The captain shifts back to us, staring out toward the pirate ship without his telescope now, wrinkles forming on his brow. While he's gazing out, the ship turns and picks up speed. He and Robert rush toward the starboard side, and I hurry after them.

"It doesn't look as if they've spotted us yet," the captain says. "They may be headed in the opposite direction we're going. In any case, we should soon be too close to port for them to risk an attack."

"It'd be better if we didn't take any chances at this point. We can't risk it. If it's the same pirate who invaded their island, not only are they in danger, but we'll have a hard fight."

My voice wants to shake as I reply, but I won't let it. "I'm afraid it's true. I'll feel much bet—"

"They're turning about," the captain breaks in with alarm. "I don't know if we can outrun them."

"Doubtful," I reply.

After muttering something inaudible under his breath, the captain turns to command his crew. "Ready the cannons."

The captain and Robert hasten toward the active crew, and I move to follow. I spot Constance hurrying on deck, and I hide behind Robert. When I peek around him, Constance is going below—toward my room, no doubt.

Robert turns to me. "You need to get below."

So it doesn't matter that Constance didn't see me, Robert is stepping in for her.

"I'll go in a moment," I say.

"You really should go now. I don't have time to discuss this."

"Then don't. I can take care of myself. Give me a sword. I can help fight if it comes down to it."

"Please just go to your cabin before they get too close." His gaze is piercing with concern, but I really will be more useful here than down below.

The captain calls for Robert, and he grunts. "Please stay safe." And then he's off.

I hasten after, not wanting to miss anything before Constance finds me. Sailors dodge around me. I don't fully know what they're doing. I've sailed before but never encountered pirates, so there was never a need to fight back. Their ship is looming ever closer, and it's turned toward us now.

Robert is speaking when I make it to him and the captain. "It looks as if they're getting ready to fire with their long guns. Brace yourselves."

A moment later, a cannon ball lands in the water, not far off the hull, sending a spray of water about. Things are getting worse. Unless I do something, we will be captured and left to the mercy of Captain Smythe.

Hoping the repercussions aren't calamitous, I lift my hand and force my magic out to change the wind heading for the pirate ship. While I'm concentrating on the task, a cannon ball rips through the main mast, sending pieces of wood flying in all directions. Just as my spell is set in motion, Robert throws me to the deck, shielding my body with his. His muscles tense, and he groans. My heart is racing.

He moves to his feet and helps me up. Shards of wood lie scattered about the deck. I take his hand, only to have small droplets of blood fall on my palm. I follow them to their source to find a gaping wound in Robert's left bicep.

"You're hurt," I say.

"It's nothing," he says and pulls me to my feet.

He drags me off toward the cabins as there's another loud splash. As we get closer, one of the sailors says, "What in the name of Bardus? Where did that squall come from, and why didn't it hit us?"

The muttering spreads across the ship, and even Robert pauses to look toward the pirate ship. My spell is working. The distance between us and the pirate ship is growing. The pirates are scrambling about, trying to adjust to the new wind.

Robert pulls me down the stairs and through the hall until we get to my room. Opening the door, we find Jocelyn frozen, her forehead creased and lip bitten. As soon as she sees me, her expression eases.

"Stay here," Robert says. His hand brushes across my arm, sending a warm trill up its length, and then he's gone.

"My lady, are you all right? Constance sent me here to wait, in case you returned before she found you. I was so worried when we couldn't locate you with the cannons going off everywhere. I was so afraid for you." Jocelyn's words fly from her mouth, and then she rushes to my side. "You're bleeding."

Fear darts through me as I glance down and see my dress covered in blood. There's no pain. Perhaps the rush of excitement keeps it at bay? I look for a wound but find nothing. By the hem of my skirt, there's a trail of red. A trail that goes out the door. My fear increases until it's a stabbing in my chest.

"It must be Robert's," I say. He's injured because he was trying to protect me. "I have to go to him."

I head for the door, but before I can leave the room, Jocelyn closes her small hand around mine, halting my progress.

"I'm sure he's fine." Her eyes are full of compassion, and her placid voice is soothing, though I still fear for Robert. "He will have taken care of it himself, or someone else will have noticed. I've been watching these soldiers, and they really take care of each other. Right now, you'll be a distraction. He'll be all right."

Though my heart says otherwise, I nod and slip down onto the bunk. The last thing I want to do is stay in here, but Jocelyn is right, and she looks as if she could use my support with all the crashing about.

As I sit, her face changes from apprehensive to serene, the wrinkles smoothing out. She taps her foot, betraying some of her tension still exists. Her unease travels to me, gnawing at my own. Robert has to be all right; he just has to.

What if he bleeds out before getting help?

It's then I realize I'm twisting my hand in my skirt—a skirt wet with blood. The red taints my hand, sending a frightening chill through my body. *Robert.*

"I—I should probably change," I say.

Jocelyn closes the door and moves to the built-in dresser. "Sorry, my lady. Worrying about your safety has left me unsettled. Here's a dress. Let me help you out of that one. It's completely ruined now. Too bad we didn't have more to bring more with us."

"Thank you, Jocelyn."

She helps me out of the soiled dress and into the fresh one.

The booming of cannon fire sounds in the distance, followed by a near splash. Neither of us speak, but I'm grateful Jocelyn is here. It's hard not to worry about Robert, Constance, and the others with the sound of danger so near, but it's easier to stay calm once Jocelyn shoves my soiled dress into a bag.

When she's finished, she sits down next to me. She is shaking so violently, I'm surprised the whole boat doesn't shake with her. I put my arm on her shoulder, hoping the action soothes her. The splashes fade in frequency and intensity. Jocelyn's shaking does as well, and my heart quietens its frantic pounding, though the worry doesn't entirely disappear. I can't get the sight of Robert's blood out of my mind.

The door bangs open, and Constance charges into the room. "Pack everything up. We're getting off this boat when we reach Port Varas. We'll walk or find a ride to Amara. We can't risk these pirates catching you. Either of you. It appears we are much too vulnerable at sea, even with your spell. Don't you give me that look; I know it was you. You shouldn't have chanced it, though no one seems to have noticed it was you."

That's Constance, knowing everything as usual. At least she's not scolding me for leaving the cabin.

Jocelyn jumps up and pulls a large bag out from under the bunk. She tears clothes from the dresser and shoves them into the bag. Emeline comes in the room and helps collect the last few things.

"I already packed our room," Emeline says.

The two girls take a seat on the bunk across from me, cramming against each other in the small space.

"I'm going to talk to the captain," Constance says. Before I can ask to go with her she adds, "You three stay here."

I suppose I could fight her—I want to know if someone attended to Robert's wound—but I don't want to cause anyone further stress. Once she leaves, noise from the crew running about reaches us. We wait in silence, the sound of cannons gone. The boat continues to rock smoothly, easing us into a sense of calm when there is none.

Several footsteps sound outside the cabin.

Robert's muffled voice comes. "I don't know what caused the advantageous wind, but it's helping. They're heading east, away from us, which is good, but we should still be cautious."

"That's what I thought," Abner replies. "We will still make for Port Varas so we can repair the mast before continuing. Constance informed me that their group will be resuming their journey on land once we reach port."

"If that is the case, I'd like to take a small number of men to escort them to their final destination," Robert says.

Abner's voice jumps in. "Rotten idea. None of us should spend more time with the elves than we have to."

"You're one to talk," Robert replies. "If you didn't have such a hate for them—"

"I think Abner may be correct," the captain interupts. "While I don't have a problem spending time with the elves, I think we should all stick together. We've already had a bad voyage. Who knows what else will happen? We can't have you leaving. Besides, you already have an injury."

"The cut didn't go as deep as it first appeared. It's bound tightly, so I barely notice." Robert's words calm me further. Thank the magic he's not further injured. I wish I could use the healing arts to help him without giving myself away. "I know you need the men, and you don't want me going, but Stewart's group has helped us. Shouldn't we do the same? We've all heard stories of what Port Varas is like. I can't in good conscience leave them with only one escort."

"They may turn their dark magic on you when your back is turned." Abner's voice is twisted in anger but softens as he continues. "I don't want to lose you, my friend. Especially not to some elves."

Robert sighs. "They won't attack me, Abner. Haven't you seen how hard they work? They're good."

Jocelyn glances up at me while the captain speaks. "I'm afraid he's right, Abner. They've only helped us, and we should return the kindness. But it goes against my better judgment to let you escort them, Robert. Your parents will have my head."

"Now that's an exaggeration. They know how stubborn I am. Besides, part of the reason I'm here is to get to know the elves better. I need to do this."

"I still say it shouldn't be, but we all know you'll go regardless. Gather two or three men. I fear that's all we can spare. I'll let Stewart know you shall accompany them."

"I'll go with him. He needs someone to watch his back," Abner says. As grateful as I am for Robert's presence, Abner is the last person I want with us, next to Captain Smythe.

"It's definitely against my better judgment to let you go," the captain says. "There are many dangers."

"But there would also be guards with us, and Robert," Abner says.

"I agree. It'd be for the best for us to stick together," Robert says. "Friends through it all. You need to be nice to them, though."

"I hate to say it, but you'd better watch your tongue, Abner, or you'll have us in a worse hole than we're in now." There's a pause from the captain followed by, "Take Jon with you. He's the best on the crew. He'll help keep everyone safe."

Silence follows, until Robert says, "It's settled, then. I'll grab Jon. We'll meet you in Amara soon."

"Be safe. We can't afford to lose you two."

"I'll keep my eye on Robert, Captain." Abner's voice is full of confidence.

Robert sighs. "We will."

Three sets of footsteps briskly fade in different directions, two down the hall and one up the stairs. I don't quite know what to think of the exchange, other than I'm grateful this won't be the last I see of Robert. Something did seem a little off about it, though. Why are Robert and Abner so important?

"This will be wonderful," Jocelyn beams. "I admit I was fearful when Constance said we'd get off at the port. I've heard stories about it that make my skin crawl. It's one of the few places I haven't traveled to yet, but never wanted to. I feel so much better about our safety with more men accompanying us."

Emeline glowers at her. "I for one think we should stay on this boat. We're comfortable here, and it will only be a few more days to Amara. Just think of all the danger we could meet by walking there."

"I'm confident Constance is making a good decision," I say. "The boat needs repair, and we don't know how long that will take. Plus, the pirates could still be there waiting. I know it's best to have an escort in Port Varas, and we'll have four. Once we're out of the port, the rest of the way should be relatively boring with no one chasing us. Maybe we'll even get a carriage or horses so we don't have to walk, though I'm looking forward to the prospect. It'll be a nice change."

Emeline glances at the floor before leaving the cabin. I hope I wasn't too short with her. And maybe she is right. I know she would be if it wasn't for the pirates, but with them around, we need to get as far as we possibly can.

I stand to go after her, but Jocelyn says, "My lady, perhaps it's best if you'd let her go. Sometimes the best thing for thinking is time alone."

"You're right. I'll be glad when this journey is over with. Though I must say I'm enjoying the adventure compared to my normally dull life."

Jocelyn grins. As long as we all remain safe, this journey will be more than worth it.

Chapter
TWELVE
⁓

T HE SEA AIR swirls around our small group as we
head down the dock. Everyone is here except Jon and
Abner, who will meet us later. A dozen or so boats
are in the process of loading or unloading cargo around us.
Sailors scamper about, most disappearing in the direction
of the closest pub. Uneasy glares come from the elves as we
pass by, the worst of which are aimed at Jocelyn, Robert, and
me—still in my human guise.

I can't determine if it's because we're human or because
we're here. I'm thinking it's both but leaning more toward
our race. I knew malcontent existed between our races, but
I didn't realize how much distrust existed among my own
people. For some foolish reason, I always thought the fault
lay with the humans.

The setting sun casts an eerie red glow across the town
square. We quicken our pace as insults are shouted our way.

The faint aroma of roast mutton from a nearby booth clings to the air, making my stomach growl. I didn't take the time to eat before we left. Perhaps it was a mistake.

Robert places his hand on the small of my back as he scouts the townspeople buying their goods. Warmth spreads throughout me as I follow his gaze. The cobblestone street remains clean through the town square, save for an elf who drops his packages at the sight of us.

I cringe. "I'm sorry about the treatment you're receiving, Robert."

He glances at me, confusion rolling out of his brown eyes. "It's not your fault."

How thickheaded of me. I might as well tell him I'm an elf. "I suppose I'm used to the behavior."

He tightens his lips into a grim line. "You shouldn't have to be used to this. You've done nothing wrong."

My heart flutters at his words, and I move to walk closer to him. Stewart, who is leading the group, sets a more vigorous pace. The air tingles with apprehension as we make our way through several more stalls until we leave the square and come upon stone houses. Elves stand whispering inside their shadowed doorways. When they meet my gaze, their eyes harden.

While Robert's touch is warming, the glares are like ice against my soul. If these elves are so upset about a small group of humans, how will they react when I marry Prince Phillip? With the extra thoughts to burden me like a pack of rocks, I watch the houses give way to dingy shacks. The cobblestone path ends, leaving only a dusty lane.

Farther down the way, we follow Stewart into an alley. The sinister heavens release their water, the consequences of my earlier spell manifesting. Not the best time for us to get soaked. The houses around us are dark. Other than our footsteps, the pattering rain is the only sound in this area of Port Varas.

Stewart leads us to some barrels and crates behind one of the houses. Hidden by the abandoned house, we get drenched in the rain while the two males converse a few feet from us in hushed tones.

"You're sure Jon and Abner knew what time to meet us?" Stewart asks.

"Yes. We should have met them back in the market. I don't know what kept them. I should go find them." Robert's voice is full of worry.

This can't be good at all. Where could they possibly be? What if those glares from the elves turned into something more?

"I'll go find them," Stewart says. "It'll be safer for me to travel through the city. Besides, I've been here before. I'll be able to track them down."

Robert follows Stewart's apprehensive gaze to me. "I'll make certain the women are safe while you're gone."

"Thank you. I'll be back shortly." Stewart gives me a nod and goes back down the alley, staying in the shadows.

Robert inches closer to me, his presence warming in the cold, wet rain. Constance stands tense, scowling at him as if he might attack at any moment.

"Stewart will find the men I sent out earlier," Robert says, ignoring her wary gaze. "I know you still don't know me, but

Stewart trusts me. Go ahead and sit. We'll stay out of this rain plaguing us as best we can."

Once I move next to the wall and sit on a crate, the other women follow. Constance peeks into the bag holding the scroll I found in the cave and readjusts the contents to keep them from getting wet, I'd guess. Then she pulls out some hard tack and hands it out to everyone—Robert last.

We eat as the pouring minutes tick by. We stand in the shadows of a building. The rain pours harder, creating large pools of water in the muddy lane. Still no sign of Stewart. We were supposed to meet the other sailors an hour ago. Worry drips from me like the rain around us.

A shuffle from the street makes everyone's muscles tense. I peek over one of the crates to find a colossal man with an elf. Fear twists in my chest.

"Captain Smythe," I whisper to the others. "What is he doing here?"

Robert shakes his head, furrowing his brow. Constance shoots me a warning look, though what she's warning me against this time, I'm uncertain. I ignore her and stretch over the crates for a second look.

"They're leaving. I think we should follow them. There's something odd about this," I say.

"*No,*" Robert and Constance whisper at the same time, but they're too late. I'm already off. They follow after me, Constance tutting at me. I turn and shake my head. Captain Smythe is already fading from view.

"We have to find out what's going on." I look pointedly at Constance.

She narrows her eyes—she doesn't like this at all—but she nods. Guilt floods me for using the command in such a situation as this, but I have to know what he's up to.

While we work to catch up without being detected, Robert mutters, "This is madness."

I cringe. I agree with him but keep moving forward. We stay as far behind the captain as we dare so we may remain undetected. Jocelyn and Emeline follow even farther behind. After several minutes, Captain Smythe and the elf enter a house. Keeping our footsteps light, we hover by the house, getting soaked.

A candle is lit, casting a dim light from the paneless window beside us. Inside, the two talk and drink, their mugs sloshing over the sound of rain when they slam them down. Their voices carry through the window. Constance motions for everyone to stand still and silent. The two voices speak casually at first, talking of looting and women, but then the conversation shifts topics.

"There were humans and elves on this ship, you say?" Captain Smythe asks. "Together?"

The second, gruffer voice answers. "Aye. Strangest thing. Don't happen much the last few years. The one human girl was sure putty, though, at least for a human. Purtiest one I've ever seen."

"Huh."

"Let's get on with this business before anyone sees me. Hate to get caught with a ruffian the likes of you."

"Ha ha ha." Sarcasm laces the fake laugh.

"Er... I meant, a fine gentleman like yourself."

"If you're quite finished, I want the ship that just came into port. We want more of it than the merchandise. I want the woman, too." Jocelyn grabs my arm, as the pirate continued. "I will pay an extra two hundred gold coins for her."

An uncomfortably long moment passes before the second voice replies, "I'm not so sure. I hate enough giving yah the ship, but people? That's another business entirely."

A booming crash comes from the house, followed by Captain Smythe's cursing. "You'll do as I say, or every elf will know of your dirty-handed business."

The second man's scream fills the air with a pain that's almost tangible. Jocelyn whimpers and squeezes my arm tighter. Robert drapes his arm across my back and pats the girl's shoulder. I mouth a *thank you* to him. He nods, angst visible in his golden brown eyes. Our gazes break apart when the screaming fades.

"Yes, yes. Whatever you want. Please donna hurt me. I'll have my men nab her when they hold up the ship. If she goes off shore, I'll have her followed. If she's already left, I know someone who can track her."

"That's more like it." Captain Smythe's voice sends chills up my arms even more than the rain is already doing. "I'll send one of my men to help you bring back the girl. The usual with the merchandise, and make it snappy. There's somewhere I need to be."

"Yes, Capin.'"

With that, the candle is blown out, and the two voices fade out of the house into the night. Jocelyn's white hand still grips me. It's probably going to leave a bruise, but all I can feel is a sick sort of numbness.

Robert looks from Constance to me uneasily, and then removes his arm from Jocelyn's shoulder and my back. I miss the warmth that he brought.

"We should head back," he says.

This time, I don't bother protesting. Of course, I don't point out I was right to protest the first time. We make our way back to the dilapidated house in silence. Jocelyn continues to cling to me. Why she picks me and not Constance is a mystery. The part of me that isn't used to being touched wants to pry her off me, but another part—a stronger, better part—wishes there was more I could do for her than let her hold my arm.

When we get back to the crates, Stewart isn't waiting for us.

"Where is he?" I ask.

Constance purses her lips and shakes her head. Which is worse? Waiting longer and not knowing what's going on, or going in search of him? Now more than ever, it's imperative that we get a move on. Before I can make up my mind what to do, Stewart appears, followed by the men he was sent after. I ease back against the house.

In a hushed voice, Robert relates what transpired while Stewart was gone. The rain feels heavier, coming so hard it's no longer drops but a full sheet of water. Robert's voice is full of concern. He keeps running his hand through his hair.

Stewart glances at me, as if to make certain I haven't been whisked away by Captain Smythe. "Change of plans," he says, when Robert is done. "We must leave at once, even though your men weren't able to acquire all the supplies. I assume you want to return to the ship and warn them?"

"I'll send Jon or Abner," Robert replies. "We'll still escort you to Amara. You have a greater need of us than the ship." He gives me a pointed look.

"I think we should go back, Robert," Abner says. "They'll be fine. They know their own country. Let's return."

"I gave them my word. You can go and warn the others. Jon and I will continue onward."

Abner scowls. "If you're going, I'm going as well. Send Jon back. I'll help you with these *elves*."

Stewart straightens to his full height, his tall frame several inches above Abner's. "We don't need the likes of you coming with us." His strong arms tense, poised as if ready to strike.

Constance rises, easing Stewart with her presence, though her face is filled with rage.

Robert slides in between the boiling sides, arms out-stretched between them.

"We don't need this. There are enough problems going around, without us adding to them. Abner, you can come with us if—and only if—you'll be more tolerant of those not like you."

Abner nods his head in agreement, but his fists remain clenched.

Robert continues. "Can you agree to this, Stewart?"

Stewart nods and eases, and Constance's harsh gaze shifts from him to Robert. Emeline and Jocelyn keep quiet and reserved.

"Jon, go and tell the captain of their danger. Make certain he knows Abner and I will still be meeting up with you in Amara."

"Yes, sir." With a nod, Jon heads down the alleyway, looking around warily as he goes, and then he disappears from sight.

"Now," Robert says, "what are we going to do about supplies? Should we try to get them or move on without them?"

"We should leave without them," I say.

"She's right," Stewart says. "There's too much danger here, and we'll be able to get supplies at Ilwen Farms. It's on the way, and I know someone there who will help us."

He looks to me for confirmation, and I give a slight nod.

"To Ilwen Farms it is," Robert says.

The group is silent as we leave town. I'll be happy not to return to Port Varas anytime soon. But as we continue on our journey, soaked to the bone, I can't help but wonder what else could go wrong.

Chapter

THIRTEEN

⌇

"WHAT CAN I do to help, Constance?" I ask. She raises her eyebrows and responds with a whisper, probably so the men can't hear. "Don't ask again."

I throw my hands up in the air. Of course I'm not used to helping, but I'm not used to doing nothing, either. With everyone else slaving away, it's more than enough to make me willing to do a few chores. But no. Constance is having none of that.

Rain continues falling mercilessly while I sit back on a stump, watching the men put together shelters for the night. They are simple, some thick canvas overhead to protect us from the rain while we sleep. Stewart and Robert fumble over the ropes. Or rather, Robert fumbles. Stewart can tie a rope without a problem, when Robert isn't trying to help.

Abner stands to the side, mouth puckered like he tasted something bad. More like he sees something he finds foul. True to his word though, he remains silent on the subject of elves.

"Will it ever stop raining?" Emeline pulls out cooking supplies. "Two days should be more than an adequate consequence."

"I'm sorry," I say. "I think I went a bit overboard with my spell on the wind."

"I'll agree to that. No one else makes it rain for this long when changing the weather."

"I—for one—like it," Jocelyn chimes in, her blond hair darkened with moisture. "It smells wonderful. Everything feels so fresh and clean. I don't mind being drenched all the time, though it did rain too hard the first night. This, though, is pure heaven."

I have to smile at the sight of her dancing in the rain, her face pointed toward the sky. She looks at me with a wide grin. I can't help but feel something in that moment. Is this what it's like to have a friend?

"That's enough playing for now." Constance's words are commanding but tinged with amusement. "Dinner needs started. Go find some firewood. Dry if you can. But stay close."

"Yes, ma'am." Jocelyn scampers around the camp but remains in view.

Constance and Emeline busy themselves making stew. Ever since Port Varas, we've been rationing our supplies carefully. Before that, even. I can't remember the last good meal I had. At least Constance is still cooking.

"I'm excited for dinner," I say to her. "It's amazing that you can find edible plants to stretch out food. I had no idea you had that kind of skill."

"I wish I could pick it up," Emeline says while stirring the stew. "I'd love to be able to make meals like Constance."

"It won't be as good tonight," Constance says. "I don't dare enhance the flavor more. The repercussion of losing some of the nutrients isn't something we can afford any longer."

"I don't mind," I say. "I'm sure it will still be good."

"It smells delicious." Emeline leans in closer to the pot in front of her.

Constance pulls back her mouth in skepticism and shifts her attention back to a tuber she is cutting. The men are still setting up a shelter. Everyone else is working. Everyone but me.

That's it. If I'm not going to work, I don't have to watch everyone else do so. I escape into the forested area. Heavily leafed branches swing at me as I walk past, spraying water. I'd grumble at the water if I wasn't already so wet. I'm so saturated the continuing rain doesn't make a difference.

I stroll on, the damp grass springy beneath my footsteps. Not wanting to get too far from camp, I slow. An itch to remove my disguise fills me. The only break I've had since our flight from danger was during the dark of night, while everyone save for the person keeping watch was asleep and my head was covered in a shawl. The amount of time I've spent as a human is sizable. If I knew the consequences for this spell, it wouldn't be so worrisome.

Out of sight of the camp, I prepare myself for the pain that will accompany changing my face back to its original form when someone yells. Although I can't understand what the voice is saying, fear leaps in my chest. I crouch down, ready to jump into action at the slightest movement. Sure, I don't have my sword, but that doesn't mean I can't jab eyeballs with my fingers.

The masculine voice calls out again but is still muffled by the pouring rain. Who is it? And where is he at? A large hand grabs my shoulder from behind, and my instincts kick in. I jam my elbow into the man's taut stomach. A grunt sounds, as I turn to face the perpetrator, ready to inflict more damage.

Robert's pain-ridden eyes stare back at me.

"I am so sorry," I say. "I thought you were someone else."

He draws in a deep breath. "I'm glad I'm not that someone else. I didn't mean to scare you. With as loud as I was yelling, I thought you would have realized I was coming. Stewart saw you wander off, and I volunteered to find you. I regret to admit my shelter-making skills are… Well, I don't have any." A playful twinkle replaces the pain in his eyes, and his chuckle is warming.

Thinking of how hard I elbowed him, heat rises to my cheeks. "I'm sorry again about attacking you. The forest was inviting, and I wanted to explore. I didn't want to disturb anyone. I suppose I'm still on edge from Port Varas."

"It'll be fine." Robert chuckles. "I can keep you company a while, but we shouldn't stray too far." He holds out an arm for me, not like a sailor, but like a courtier.

I slip my arm through the opening and place my hand on his forearm. We walk through the woods in silence. The trees around us are thick with gold, orange, red, and a few green leaves. Moisture clings along each leaf's five points, until we brush past, knocking it off. Rain drops lessen as we head under an unusually heavy canopy.

Two deer stand close by when we abate our progress, but they don't seem bothered by us. I'd been looking forward to letting my disguise down, knowing I'll have to keep it up for a couple weeks, but spending time with Robert is worth it. Still, I am a betrothed woman. Even though I don't know the man I'm to marry, I shouldn't disrespect him. The happiness I've found dampens at the thought.

"Tell me, what is your prince like? I don't know much about him."

"He's your prince too. Not many people know much about him, though. He doesn't go out among the people much."

I scowl. Why wouldn't he? I do at least every once in a while. "That's too bad. He should enjoy meeting with the people."

"It's just what I've heard." He tilts back on the heel of his foot, not looking me in the eye. "It may very well not be true. Though I saw him once, and he seemed caring. He started walking among the people, but some official came over to him. They appeared to be having an argument about something. After that, he left. I suppose it could have been some other pressing business, but he looked at the gathered crowd with such a longing."

"I hope it is true. If I were to lead the country, I'd spend time with the people."

"I would, too. The royalty are only concerned with themselves." At his words, a thrill of connection shakes through me.

He sits down on a log and continues. "They should take time to find out what's really happening with the commoners and work to make it better."

"Do you not consider yourself a commoner, as a sailor?"

"I suppose I should, but my family does fine. They trade with Captain Zaccheus often. That's how I came to be under him. I convinced him to let me sail with them for the time being. My mother was against the idea, but I wanted a change. The captain understands my need to get away from my parents and talked her into the idea."

"He sounds like a good man."

Robert smiles. "He is. Since I was a little boy, whenever he would come to trade with my parents, he would teach me something. Fencing, boxing, things about the life of a sailor... He even taught me how to eat at a formal dinner and how to dance."

"Captain Zaccheus?" I try to picture the old seaman dancing, but the image refuses to come.

"Yes." Robert laughs. "I have no siblings, so he would take the woman's part. I can still hear his voice giving directions in a high pitch."

I laugh, full force. "I have to see that."

"Perhaps we can make that happen sometime."

"I would really like that."

We fall into a comfortable lull while the rain drips around us until I think about the information I gleaned about Prince Phillip. He may turn out all right, if Robert's observation is correct. In any case, the peace my marriage to him will bring is no longer what my heart yearns for. Love is what I want. Something like the attraction for Robert that continues to grow within me.

Where did that thought come from? It could lead to much danger. I watch him from the corner of my eye and resist the urge to either touch him or run away from him. I'm a betrothed princess. Even if I wasn't betrothed, marrying a common sailor would never be condoned.

I want to growl in frustration. It's not fair. If I let my heart continue down this path, I'll have to give up the crown. There is no other heir to the throne if I leave, and I don't know what would happen to the country I love. Frustrated, I sit on the bumpy log next to Robert. My hand brushes his.

I should pull my hand away. I will pull my hand away.

Only, before I can do so, he leans closer.

My breath becomes shallow and catches in my throat. A flame kindles in my heart. It's small at first, but then bursts into a blaze coursing through my body. I tilt my face toward his, and time ceases to exist as I'm aware of nothing but Robert.

My own breathing matches the rapid rise and fall of his chest. I can't help but take him in, from his chiseled jaw line all the way to his distinguished brow. From his angular nose to a small scar above his mouth—a sharp line that cuts across a portion of his upper right lip. I'd noticed it before, but never paid much attention to it.

Now it consumes me. My fingers want to touch it. My lips want to brush against it.

We stay locked in a halfway almost-there-but-not-quite kiss. With his strong arms, he pulls me in closer. The warmth of his body fills me, fighting against the chill in the air. His lips hover just above mine. He reaches up and strokes my face.

As we gaze into each other's eyes, I melt into him, losing myself. The spell I cast on my eyes falters, and they change to their true hue.

Stiffing a cry of pain, I bend my head down and reactivate the spell. My eyes fill with tears from the stinging, but they'll no longer appear as my own. The crushing ache is much worse in my chest, though I can't tell if it's from not kissing him or almost doing so.

I pull myself back up to find Robert's brows drawn together under a creased forehead. He moves back, lets go of my hand, and stands. The air around us fills with awkward tension.

"We should get going." His words hold no emotion.

The walk back is silent, leaving me cringing with every step. The rain grows cooler. At the beginning of our stroll, he had led me on his arm like a gentleman. Now a wide gap surges with unease between us.

The sound of people moving and talking fills the air. Without a word, we both slow until we come to a standstill. We face one another, Robert looking apprehensive. His gaze shifts about, everywhere but at me. Finally, he settles his gaze on me, and his face softens.

"Adelei"—his voice is tender, but it feels wrong not hearing him say my true name—"I'm sorry."

"Don't be sorry. I must confess something. You see"—I take a deep breath for courage—"my hand is already promised to another."

I turn and rush for the presence of others. My chest compresses painfully, and one small tear slides down my cheek.

Chapter
FOURTEEN

❧

THE WARM SUNLIGHT embracing me is a welcome change. The rain stopped just this morning, and it was wonderful to be able to enjoy dry clothes. I lean against a smooth rock and massage my aching feet. They aren't used to such abuse.

Other than three tiring days, the trip so far has proven uneventful.

The clearing I'm in is small but cozy. Maple trees surround it in a tight weave, save for three spots where they break. One of those spots heads back to the direction of our temporary camp. The occasional twang of metal echoes across the woods as my servants pack up.

The snap of a twig from behind makes me jump and look about. Seeing nothing, I settle back down on the small patch of dirt. I pull my legs up in front of me, close my arms around them, and bury my head into my knees.

Clenching my jaw for the expected pain, I let the magic spell on my face release but leave the blond hair. Once the sharp pain subsides, it feels good to be myself again.

Free from distractions, my mind wanders to what I've been trying to avoid since yesterday. Robert's closeness. The warm tingling when my fingers slid across his face. The potent desire in my heart when his lips hovered mere inches from mine is vivid. How I ached to kiss them. Who cares if I'm betrothed to Prince Phillip, anyway?

Tears fill my eyes and splash down on my knees.

Not knowing how soon Constance will appear, I stifle them. I concentrate on the rustling of the leaves around me while letting the tears dry. A sweet-smelling breeze brushes across my skin.

The crunch of footsteps toward me. I peek through the small crack between my knees.

Looking at home in the woods around her, Constance strolls forward. "Isn't it nice to have a break? Especially from the rain." She sits down next to me and leans against the bolder. "How are you feeling, my lady? I'm sorry we weren't able to procure a better means of transportation for you."

A false laugh escapes me, muffled by my legs. "Don't worry for me. I'll be fine, though I may have several blisters on my feet by the time we reach Amara. This has been a good break. I only wish we weren't running for safety, but instead taking a leisurely trip."

"I agree with that. As much as I enjoy being out in nature, I'll feel more at peace when we have you back at the castle. I don't know what your parents were thinking, sending you all the way to Sulamay without a detachment of guards. Even if they wanted to send you in secrecy, they should have provided more protection."

"They were trying to keep me safe, but I think you're right. I wonder what has happened to the guard they were supposed to send."

"I'm sure we'll find out soon enough."

"We will." I pause, unsure how to broach the topic I want to discuss with her. "Ha—Have you ever been in love?"

She looks closer at me, scrutinizing my face. Finally she looks away and answers, "Once."

"Will you tell me about it?"

With a deep sigh, she says, "It was before you were born. His name was Andries. We met while I was on an errand for your mother. She insisted on having a new horse, though she hardly used her current one. I went to the stables where Andries worked. He helped me choose an animal that would be suitable for the queen, all the while talking and jesting."

"You? Shy?"

Constance laughs. "It's hard to imagine, but I was. Our conversation covered every topic. We disagreed on a great many things, but he was a gentleman always, and let me have my opinion with grace.

"I was young then, though older than you are now, so I was approaching the age where spinsterhood was upon me. It was something I feared back then. When he continued showing interest, I was not only flattered, I held on to the hope that he would ask for my hand."

Constance pauses, her face pulled down and tears glistening in her eyes. I've never seen such emotion from her before. It leaves me not knowing what to say or do. I should have asked her more questions sooner. I take advantage of her motherly position too often, never taking the time to get to know her better. I keep my gaze on her, not wanting to miss anything while she finishes her narrative with a melancholy tone.

"It was then your mother heard of his attention to me. She flew in the kitchen one night—the first and only time I've ever seen her there. She was livid and demanded Andries leave immediately. He stood up to her, the lone person who has done so other than your father. Right there, he declared his love for me and his intention of marrying me.

"I think you have been told, but your parents tried desperately to produce an heir to the throne. They were unsuccessful until then. She demanded I choose between her and Andries. Though my love for him was deep, I couldn't leave. I knew that when your mother bore her child, the babe would need me."

She looks at me, as I'm still barely peeking out from behind my limbs. "And you have," she says. "Your dear mother, bless her, didn't know from the start what to do with a child. I knew the importance of rearing the heir to the throne. Andries understood better than I thought he would. I missed his company at first, but you soon filled all my time."

This is not where I expected the conversation to go. "I had no idea. I'm so sorry."

"Don't be, my dear. You are the jewel of my life now."

Heat flushes my cheeks. "What happened to Andries?"

"I've found information about him when I could. He never did marry. He spends most of his time traveling, even spending time with humans."

"I didn't think any elf would choose to do that."

Constance grins. "He always was fascinated with the history of our two cultures. I plan on getting the scroll you found to him, somehow. Andries is the most knowledgeable elf I know with historical items. He traded his love for horses for his love of the past after we parted."

"I'd like to meet him."

"I don't know if your mother would make an allowance for it." She purses her lips. "As for right now, there's something I want to talk to you about."

That doesn't sound good. "What is it?"

"I'm a trifle worried about you. You've been wearing that human guise so long, I'm afraid the consequences may be harsh, whatever they are. It may be the blond hair I'm not used to, though."

"I've worried about this myself, but I can't think of a better way to get home."

Her forehead wrinkles with worry, her face showing a hint of her true age. She knits her hands together, a sign I know to mean she's thinking deeply.

Not wanting to disturb her train of thought, I sit silent, feeling the apprehension in the air.

At length, Constance speaks. "We shall have to keep a close eye on you. I don't know what to expect from you anymore. My predictable little girl has grown into an unpredictable woman. Ah, such is life. There were still a few things left to pack up. I'm going to make sure they were done properly, and then we'll be ready to go. Will you be coming with me now?"

"No. I think I will enjoy not having a human face for a bit longer."

"I should have guessed as much. Don't dawdle too long."

Constance heads off, and I can't help but call after her. "Thank you for sharing your story with me."

She nods and strides toward the small camp with a purpose. Her words about not knowing what to expect from me bubble up. Is there more I can do with my power that I haven't yet discovered? I don't know how to find out or where to even begin, but maybe more will reveal itself with time and practice.

A cool breeze picks up from the north, tossing my hair about my face. The disguise that was fun at first is now growing old. I can't wait to be rid of it and have my own dark hair back. With a wince, I change my face back to the human one and release my legs.

A foul stench fills my nose, gagging me. I sit up straight and reach up to cover my nose. Before I can do so, a dirty hand wraps around my face, covering my mouth. There's no time to react. My attacker has me caught like a fish.

I hit and kick behind me, connecting with my attacker, but he doesn't let go. With more strength than I can fight, he drags me farther from camp.

"Adelei," Robert calls from close by. "Adelei?"

My attacker spins me around. He leers at me, his yellowed teeth bared as he pulls out a knife as dirty as he is.

My muscles tense. If there's a way out of this, I'll find it. "*Robert,*" I scream.

The pirate strikes me on the temple with such force, I fly to the ground. My head throbs, my vision blurring. Knowing the pirate is still close by, I roll away. A filthy hand grabs my arm, forcing me to stay close. Through my unclear sight, I see Robert barreling at my attacker.

Robert's heavy blows dislodge the pirate's firm grip on me. I scramble clear of his reach. The two men struggle for control, the knife between them. Robert is bigger, but his bicep is still injured from the boat.

He swings at the pirate, but the pirate blocks him before his fist can make contact. The knife falls to the ground. The pirate kicks toward Robert's right knee. With an angry mutter, Robert darts back. A wicked laugh comes from the pirate, who hurtles himself at Robert.

I eye the forgotten knife left behind.

The men fling themselves together again, this time appearing to embrace like old friends, except for the contorted looks upon their faces. Robert is gaining the upper hand, when they fall to the ground. They wrestle, tumbling closer to me as I reach for the knife. The movement happens so fast, I can't get out of the way. The pirate's leg swings into my stomach while he attempts to eradicate himself from Robert.

I clutch my stomach, attempting to hold in the pain. The pirate searches along the ground, feeling for the knife but finding a rock. Still woozy from the blow, I grab a large stick and hurl it at him, aiming for his face.

The stick connects, giving Robert the chance to grab the rock out of the pirate's hand. Robert clobbers the pirate on the side of the head with it and knocks him out cold.

Beads of sweat dripping from his brow, Robert looks up at me, eyes wide with concern. "Are you all right?"

It's still awkward between us, even as I struggle to reign in the pain. Tension clings to the air from my unease and the exhausting fight. "Yes, thanks to you. I'm certain this is one of Captain Smythe's crew. He looks familiar."

Robert nods. "Run and grab Stewart so he can help me bring back this scoundrel and scout for others that may be about."

I nod, grateful to get away—though from the pirate or the awkwardness around Robert, I'm not sure. I turn and dart back to camp, an ache in my side.

Chapter
FIFTEEN

∾

I CAN'T HELP BUT laugh when Constance throws cold water on the smelly pirate. He stands, sulking, while his bound wrists and Stewart's hold on his arms keep him from running. He stares at everyone with dark, murderous eyes.

"Really." Constance sniffs at him to see if he's fit for travel yet. "How can you stand to be around yourself with that stench?"

"*Argh.*" The angry noise sounds more like an animal's than a person's.

Stewart tightens his large hands, but Constance goes about finishing the job as if nothing happened.

Robert and Stewart thoroughly searched the area but were unable to locate others that might be following us. Once again, no one is allowed to go off alone, in case someone else is out there.

Jocelyn and Emeline finish packing away the few items Constance used to clean the pirate, and everyone is ready to wind their way through the forest. Sometime this afternoon, we'll get fresh supplies. The prospect makes me want to walk faster.

The leaves are perfectly still as we continue on our journey. The day promises to be a warm one. A few high, puffy clouds are the only thing gracing the sky besides the radiating sun. Birds chirp their noisy song in the forest around us.

My legs ache from all the exertion of walking the past several days. Relaxing walks are fine, but this is grueling. Everyone else manages to keep a good pace. They are even dragging along the pirate, whose hands are bound. With my lungs burning, I slow to a stop and cringe.

Robert turns and looks back at me. Heat rises to my face. He leans over and whispers something in Stewart's ear. They speak a moment, with Stewart shaking his head several times and looking at me. Robert's mouth moves one last time, and then he heads toward me. Constance glances back, eyes tightening.

"She's fine." Stewart interrupts the silence. "Robert will make sure she's all right. We'll slow our pace a little, but we have to keep moving."

Constance's eyes fill with worry, but she turns and continues on, as does the rest of the group. Robert hands me a water pouch. Still feeling awkward around him, I'm not sure I like this arrangement. I take a long, refreshing drink. I'm uneasy as I look about the dense forest around us, avoiding Robert's gaze.

"Are you doing well?" he asks.

"Yes, thank you. I'm not accustomed to so much strenuous walking. I'll be fine."

"Do you think you can keep going? Or should I carry you?"

My cheeks flame. Which is the worse prospect? Continuing to walk and ache, or being humiliated by being carried by him? Admittedly, being carried does have a certain appeal to it. "I can keep going."

So we walk behind the group, slowly, but at least we're moving forward. My face still burns as I concentrate on walking in an attempt to rid myself of it.

We set a steady pace, still faster than what I'm used to, but not the brisk pace that's beyond my stamina.

"By later today we should be there, and then we can eat a filling meal and rest up," Robert says.

"That sounds wonderful, especially if Constance is cooking."

"Agreed." He hesitates, but then pushes on. "I didn't wish to make you uncomfortable, and I would have left you alone had I known of your impending marriage."

Fearing to speak what I actually want to say, I simply nod and keep placing one foot in front of another. Marriage to a prince wouldn't be nearly as nice as getting to know Robert better.

We continue in silence for a time, and my discomfort gradually diminishes. The walking is no longer as hard. The ground remains fairly even though my legs burn with the effort. I concentrate on my footsteps, avoiding rocks and branches along the thin grass path.

"Tell me more about your intended." Robert breaks the silence. "I didn't know servants were allowed such luxuries until they'd been released from duty in the royal courts."

I grab a hold of my skirt. "Ah, well, I suppose you found an exception. As you can see, I still belong to Princess Arabella. She gave…consent for my marriage. Though she doesn't appear to like it." I mumble the last line knowing I shouldn't say such things, but wanting to anyway.

"Humph." His nose wrinkles with disgust and then smoothens out. "Tell me about the lucky fellow."

I try to hide yet another blush by glancing in the other direction while I spin out a lie I hate to tell. "There's not really much to tell. I'm mostly following Constance's wish for me to marry and be provided for. She loves her own job but doesn't feel it's a lifelong task for me. I'll still be there for the Princess on important occasions."

He sighs deeply. "When is the wedding to take place?"

Caution spreads through me. "I'm not sure how things are going to go at this point. Everything has been so crazy lately."

"It sure has. Will you still be with Princess Arabella for her wedding?"

"I don't think I'll ever stray too far from the Princess's side." I laugh bitterly. "What about yourself? What great plans do the future hold?"

Asking about him will keep me from lying but won't protect my heart. What can he tell me that won't make him more desirable?

Instead of answering, he looks at the group ahead of us and says nothing. We walk a few miles like this, the group getting further as we go, though staying in sight. The silence is only interrupted by the padding of our feet. An air of uneasiness hovers about as if waiting to suffocate us.

Remembering Constance's words about Andries, I wonder how my relationship to Robert compares to it. Constance had mentioned disagreements. Was this what she meant? Not that this relationship is like what Constance described. But there's a feeling of promise to it. Like it could become so if we'd only let it.

It doesn't feel like we're arguing, but we're not talking. Maybe it's the same thing. I don't know why I care anyway. He shouldn't be too familiar with me now that he knows of my wedding. He's probably not interested in any case.

I concentrate on the pain to avoid more thoughts of him. My legs had been like rubber upon waking this morning, even shaking when I stood. That had been bad, but this was worse. Not only dd they feel like rubber, but they feel like they are on fire now.

When the group ahead of us gets out of sight, they stop and wait until we get almost caught back up. I take a long draw from the water skin, quenching my thirst. The side of my stomach groans in protest. I grab my side, squeezing in an attempt to ease the pain. Instead, I hit the bruise caused by the pirate when he kicked me. A moan of pain escapes me. Robert glances over and then quickly looks back at the road.

The pain from my side reminds me of the earlier fight. I'm certain my face looks atrocious. Without a mirror, I haven't seen the bruise myself, but with Constance wincing every time she glances my way, it has to be bad. Thankfully, it only hurt when I touch it.

I watch Robert out of the corner of my eye. He doesn't appear to be any worse off after the fight, though he favors his uninjured arm whenever he moves tree branches out of our way.

Glancing at the pirate ahead of us, it's easy to see he hadn't fared so well. He limps visibly. The cut on his head is deep. Constance had done an overly good job bandaging it. I have to wonder if she went overboard on purpose.

Constance had considered healing us all, at least me and Robert, but Stewart insisted that everyone needed to save their strength. Though Constance had tried to disobey Stewart by drawing on her own health to heal me, I stopped her, not wanting to deplete Constance's health in favor of my own.

My breathing comes in har,d and we slow even more. I can't stand this any longer. "I'm sorry if I said something that offended you. I was only making conversation."

He rubs a finger over his eyebrow and replies as if the conversation had never stopped. "Don't be sorry. I'm not offended. It's a difficult subject for me. My parents and I don't exactly see eye to eye. To them, my future is perfectly mapped out, but for me," he sighs, "it's not so well planned. This is one reason I'm grateful for this chance to get away from them for a while."

"Ah, yes. Parents. I'm sorry to hear you're having problems with them. I hope they can be resolved."

"I hope for it too, but we'll see." He offers me a half-smile.

"What are your parents like? Other than seeing a different future for you."

"They are…well, I guess they're good people. I fear I'm biased on the subject while I'm not getting along with them."

"What exactly don't you agree on?" I'm prying, but I can't stop myself from asking.

"My father wants me to follow in his footsteps and take on the family business. Sailing appeals to me more, though."

"What does your father do?"

Robert's forehead wrinkles, his mouth pulling into a frown. "He's a merchant."

"I remember now. You said your family trades with Captain Zaccheus."

"Yes. I shouldn't speak ill of my parents, but they're too greedy. I don't want to be like them, in that regard at least." His voice is sour, but as he continues, it becomes wistful. "Sorry. I really shouldn't have said that even if I do think it's true. It's easy to talk to you, though."

"I'm glad you think so. Your parents do sound difficult to be around. I can't blame you for wanting an escape. You don't have to worry about being like them, though. You've only been generous to me."

"I'm glad to hear someone thinks so. I worry…" He shakes his head. "It's funny. You seem to understand, yet you're an orphan, and the closest thing to parents for you are Constance and Stewart. They are nothing like my parents."

I laugh, trying to keep it light. "They certainly are not. I—"

Before I can finish my thoughts, my foot catches on a protruding branch, sending me flying to the ground. Robert wraps his arm around my waist, pulling me back up before I crash into the hardened dirt below.

I look up at him, our bodies touching. My breath had been whisked from me, though not from the fall, and I'm trying to find it again. But it won't seem to come.

His arms slowly move from around me, ending by his side, but our bodies remain next to each other. Our gazes lock, warmth flowing through me. I want to lean in close and fall again, this time purposefully into his arms.

But I can't. Not ever.

Slowly, but somehow much too quickly, I pull back. My waist still tingles though his arms are no longer there. The all too familiar heat fills my face as I linger on his touch.

"Th—Thank you," I finally manage to stutter out.

He nods, but says nothing. With an unsaid agreement, we both start walking again, only this time remaining silent. The bond circulating between us is almost tangible, intensifying with each step.

Chapter
SIXTEEN

༄

AFTER ANOTHER HOUR of walking in the oddly stimulating silence, the daylight faded. We are half a mile from Ilewen Farms. Exhaustion pounds at me by the time we reach the others already setting up camp. Constance insisted that we eat and get a good night's sleep before we go for supplies. I'm more than willing to follow the plan if it means I don't have to walk more for the moment. Though it does mean eating a meal that leaves my stomach grumbling. I settle into the shelter, ground cold and hard beneath me.

I awake the next morning to my entire body aching. I roll over and cover my eyes with my hand as the bright light bombards me. Blinking several times, I finally sit up and drop my hand. The now familiar smell of campfire drifts to me. I stand and quickly dress.

Constance greets me at the fire with a bowl of mush. "It's not much, but it'll get you through the day."

"Thank you." I accept the bowl and eat the thin cereal quickly as Emeline and Jocelyn clean up everyone else's breakfast. They hover over the scowling pirate. I scrape the last of the white mixture out of my bowl and hand it to Emeline's waiting hand.

"We should get going. I want to get supplies and try to be back early so we can get another good night's rest in before finishing our journey," Stewart said. "We should leave the prisoner behind until we've scouted out the town. Robert, Abner, would you please stay with him?"

"We will," Robert answered for them both.

"Thank you. Constance, are you going or staying?"

"I'll come with. Adelei should come as well."

I grind my teeth at the thought of more walking, but try to cover it with a smile. I'm certain Constance is just worried about me. That, or my being with Robert is bothering her. Not that there's an issue there. At least not one I'll let anything happen with. Still, the forced smile leaves my face.

"I'd like to join you as well, if permitted. It'd be nice to see some of Ilewen Farms again," Jocelyn says.

"That's fine," Stewart says and then turns to Emeline. "As long as you're able to finish cleaning camp?"

"I can handle it. There's not much left to do, and it means I won't have to walk."

I can't help the twinge of jealousy that comes at that.

"After everything is cleaned up, take some time for yourself," Constance tells her.

Emeline replies with a grin. "Thank you, ma'am."

Those of us going to Ilewen Farms turn and follow Stewart toward town. At least it's not far to go today. As we leave camp, a sense of unease creeps over me. The sensation grows when I glance back at the camp that was hidden from view by the trees.

I hope it doesn't have anything to do with Robert. Or maybe that is what's causing it. I don't want to think on it too hard. Brushing the feeling off like an unwelcome bug, I continue walking. This time, we take a slower pace, making it easy for me to keep up, though it still makes my feet ache.

"Stewart," I interrupt the silence. "Would you tell me about the man we're going to see? How do you know you can trust him?"

"He's my father. If we can't trust him, I don't know who we can trust."

"Oh." The heat of the day is growing, bearing down on me. "Why haven't I met him before?"

Constance answers the question with a laugh. "He's too busy for anyone, even royalty. Since I've known him, he keeps mostly to himself with work."

"Will he be upset with us for coming, then?" Jocelyn asks.

"Not when he sees me," Stewart says. "Though my father is constantly at work trying to keep Ilewen Farms in good order, he always makes time for me. Once he hears of our plight, I'm sure he'll try to do more than we need him to."

"He sounds like a good man." I wipe the sweat off my forehead with the back of my hand. "I'm sure I could convince my parents to give him some help so he doesn't have to overwork himself."

"I've already tried. The man persists in doing everything himself. He has some assistance, but he always refuses their

help. He feels that if he doesn't do it, it won't get done right."
Stewart laughs harder this time.

"Here we are."

Golden grain crops sway in the gentle breeze, contrasted
by the bright-blue sky. The sight of elves busy at work in
the fields brings back memories of my previous visits here.
Usually I came after the harvest was brought in, to celebrate
the year's crops. The celebration would last three days, with
all the elves staying up late into the night.

On the first day, my parents and I would inspect the year's
growth. The second day, a competition would be held, where
twenty elves from all over Omanska would try to bake their
best bread. On the third day, the queen would sample every
bread and declare a winner. The winner would then make
dinner for the royal family, all while festivities continued.
The food was always good, but not as good as Constance's.

Now it must be harvest time. Males and females worked
alongside each other in the crowded fields. I've never seen so
many people in the fields before. They stand to watch us walk
by. Instead of the looks of revere I normally receive, looks of
contempt shoot in my direction. I quicken my steps to remain
close to Stewart. Jocelyn keeps near as well, while Constance
brings up the last of the group.

"Does it take much longer to get there?" I ask Stewart.

"We're close."

"Good. These stares are giving me the creeps."

"They are a little more troublesome than I expected, even
having two humans with us."

It must be bad if he's worried about it.

"They weren't this bad when I came before," Jocelyn says.

"That's because you were with the princess," Constance replies. "Being with her has protected you from a lot, my dear girl."

Nearing the center of the farming community, we see the giant wooden warehouse used for storing grain until it can be shipped to its destination. Gathered around the building is a huge group of elves talking in lowered voices. Many of the females are brushing tears off their wet faces. As we pass through the group, several malicious looks are sent to me and Jocelyn, but unlike in Port Varas, no insults are hurled our way.

Stewart leads us through the group and is about to enter the building, when a snatch of conversation reaches me, stopping me in my tracks. Jocelyn tumbles into my back, but I barely notice.

"I bet it was one of those humans that took the princess. Good for nothing they are."

"Those stupid humans. I bet it was them who took Princess Arabella, trying to get out of joining our countries. They think they're so much better than us and will do anything. I say good riddance to them. We don't need them," an old lady crackles.

Frozen, I stare at the two females. They both notice me, and their faces fill with scowls of disgust.

"What right do you think you have to look at us, human?" the first lady spits out.

"I—I am sorry. I just… Did I hear you wrong? Did you say someone took Princess Arabella?"

Stewart moves back by me now.

"Yes, you halfwit. Where have you been?" the second lady answers. "The king sent word out, and everyone has been searching for her."

The first nods in agreement. "Some type of note was sent to King Sterling and Queen Pernilla, but no one knows what it says. The princess hasn't been seen since. I'm sure some brutish human the likes of you two had something to do with it."

If only they knew who they were talking to. What must my parents be thinking? They must be frantic. Clearly the whole country is in an uproar. We have to return as soon as we can.

Stewart steps protectively in front of me and Jocelyn. "You two had best be moving on. These two girls aren't hurting anyone." Without waiting for a reply, he urges us into the building, leaving the crowd behind.

We keep walking forward, following Stewart again, eyes adjusting to the dim warehouse. The dark building is full of crates stacked high on top of each other. As I can see, it seems they never end.

I glance at Constance, who is walking calmly but kneads her hands together. This situation is stressful on everyone.

Stewart leads us through a maze of crates and stops at a well-hidden door. When he pulls it open, brilliant light pours into the dark storage room. We file into the small white room.

An elf sits at a wooden desk, filling out paperwork that flows onto the floor and scatters about the room. Though the area is crowded by our small group trying not to step on papers, he doesn't appear to notice our presence. A wide window behind him lets the light in, making it hard to define his features. Only one wooden chair sits in front of the cluttered desk, though it looks as if it might break with the slightest breeze.

Stewart motions for me to sit in the worn chair. Fearing it won't hold even my small frame, I shake my head. Firmly, he takes a hold of my shoulders and prods me into the chair. It groans angrily at my weight but manages to hold steady.

The noise of the chair stirs the man to life, who looks up at our group. His expression is still hidden by the light of the window, but I see wiry hair sticking out at random places. The man's hand is poised to write something down on one of the many papers strewn about.

He looks toward Stewart then drops his pen and jumps up to greet him with a hug. "Stewart, my boy. I almost didn't recognize you, covered in all the dirt."

"I'm sorry to interrupt you, Father. I know how busy you are."

Stewart's father sits back down in his chair and moves his hand in the air like he's brushing something off. "Nonsense. I can always make time for you."

"Father, you already know Constance. These two girls are traveling with us. Ladies, this is my father, Lothair."

"Pleasure to meet you, ladies." Lothair tips his head. "What brings you here?"

He's the first elf to look at us like we're elves and not humans. It's a good change of pace.

"We need help. We're on a secret mission. More than I thought we would. We are headed to Amara and will need fresh supplies, but more importantly, we have some very precious cargo with us that is in more danger every moment we delay."

"What precious cargo?" Lothair's baritone resonates through the small room.

Stewart looks at me, a question shining through his eyes. I nod my consent, and he moves to the large window and pulls down the yellowing curtains. Instantly, the room is filled with darkness. Lothair lights a lantern, illuminating everything. Shadows dance across the wrinkles on his face. The gray-blue eyes remind me of Stewart. His face has seen many years, but a kindness softens his features.

With the light concentrated on me, I let the human disguise melt off and my true self shine forth. A whimper escapes my lips. My companions murmur as the light dances on my elven face. Without a word, the man gets off his chair, moves around the desk, and kneels in front of me, head bowed. He gently places his wrinkled hand upon my own.

"My lady." His voice is barely audible but filled with awe. "I'm so glad to know you're safe. In what way can I assist you?"

"You may rise, good sir," I say. "We are in need of the supplies Stewart told you of. Enough of them to get us to Amara. Also, just outside of town, with our group, there's a prisoner who needs to be held discreetly."

"Why not drop this disguise and travel as yourself? The people will surely be glad to see you. They'll hold no danger to you once they realize you aren't human."

"There's a hidden danger," Stewart says. "The king and queen sent us to Sulamay Island because of a threat on Princesss Arabella's life. A detachment of guard was supposed to follow shortly. They never arrived. Instead, Captain Smythe and his men came."

Lothair's mouth falls open with a gasp. "How did you survive?"

"As you can see, the princess is quite clever. She was able to avoid detection. I'm unsure why they didn't do more harm to us; there is something odd about it. But we were able to catch a ship headed for Amara. It was attacked by the same pirates. We made an escape but were chased down by the pirate who is now our prisoner. Something is wrong. I don't know if we're still being chased, or what to expect upon arrival in Amara. The princess best remain in hiding until we figure out what's going on."

Lothair's face scrunches together in worry, his gaze shifting between me and Stewart. "This is troublesome news. I will make arrangements, my lady. I wish I could go with you, but I'm afraid that would only draw more attention to you. I'll have my most trusted men go with you instead to retrieve the prisoner. They won't know of your true identity, though, Princess. I fear if you are to go parading about as a human, you won't be treated kindly."

"I understand. The disguise isn't something I can change, but the attitude is one I hope to." I didn't realize how much I wanted to change it until just this second, but I do. Innocent humans shouldn't have to travel through our lands in fear. "For now, though, we will deal with it."

"Yes, my lady. Go ahead and change into your guise. What an amazing talent you have. I wish that we could wait for the guard. Don't you think we should?"

"The sooner we get her home, the better," Stewart says. "The guard was already supposed to arrive once and failed.

I'm not trusting them again. Besides, with pirates about and humans being cantankerous against elves, they're spread thinly as it is."

"Ah, my boy, you know best. I will see to your supplies."

He moves to the door with surprising speed and vanishes without a sound. Letting my magic place the human form back upon me with a cringe of pain, I nod for Stewart to open the curtains.

We wait in silence. Jocelyn's shifting from one leg to the other is the only movement in the room. I don't dare shift in the rickety chair. About ten minutes later,, the door opens again and Lothair walks through followed by two stocky fellows with packs on.

"Sorry for the delay. These two elves, Stephen and Brendan, will escort your prisoner back here, where we will keep him until further notice. They are carrying enough supplies to get you to Amara, but you will have to carry them once back at camp."

I'm so anxious for good meals, I'd carry both packs myself.

"We greatly appreciate all that you have done for us," I say.

"I assure you, the pleasure has been all mine. I only wish I could do more. Next time I see you, son." He clasps Stewart's shoulders and pulls him close for a brief hug before letting go.

We head out the door with the two bulky elves following us out of the dark building. We make our way through the large crowd, but with the new elves with us, we receive only a few nasty looks and are able to quickly head out of town.

As we near camp, an uncomfortable feeling rises in my chest. Stewart must sense it too because he increases his long stride. We are almost jogging to keep up with him, my legs screaming in protest. I keep reminding myself it isn't far now.

We enter camp, and everything appears normal, until I'm struck by the thought that no one can be seen in camp. A twinge of fear bolts through me.

Chapter
SEVENTEEN

◠

S TEWART RUSHES IN front of me, knees bent, sword
drawn. I should have included my own sword in the list
of supplies. The two elves that joined us drop the supplies to the ground and also draw their swords.

"Robert," Stewart calls out. "Emeline. Abner. Robert?"

His voice echoes through the trees, and the leaves appear
to shake from his voice as the wind rustles them. The frightful
silence that follows each shout chills me to the core. Jocelyn
scoots her thin frame closer to me. Seeing the younger girl's
fright, I reach out and grab her hand. The girl's terror becomes
even more apparent when she squeezes my hand so hard it
hurts.

Stewart opens his mouth to call out again when there's a
thumping noise to the side of camp. Stephen and Brendan
hold their weapons at the ready and slink over to investigate
the noise. My heart pounds as they move toward the gather-

ing of maple trees and the side of camp and disappear. What if it's an ambush? Now more than ever I want my sword.

"It's all right," Brendan calls. "There are three people back here all tied up. Two male humans and a female elf."

"That would be part of our group. Go ahead and untie them and bring them out. I'll make sure camp is secure."

Stewart looks at Constance, nodding his head toward me, and moves to do a thorough investigation of the camp. Constance hovers protectively over me while we wait for the others to come into the clearing.

Emeline is the first to emerge. Though dirt and weeds covers her clothes, she appears no worse for the wear. Her scowl deepens as she stretches out her body. Jocelyn releases her grip on my numb hand and goes to fuss over Emeline.

After a few moments, both Robert's and Abner appear, followed closely by the two elves. Both the elves and Abner hold distrustful looks, but Robert is visibly relieved when he sees us. As he speaks with Stewart, he keeps glancing at me.

"I apologize. I've no idea how he could have escaped. One minute he was tied up and the next he had Emeline with a sword to her throat, threatening to cut it." I gasp, and he continues, tone softer, "Fearing for her life, we did as he wanted. He made Abner tie up Emeline and me, and then he tied up Abner. After making sure we couldn't go anywhere, he ran off. It didn't look like he headed for town, but I was afraid he went after you."

Stewart puts his hand on Robert's shoulder, lifting Robert's gaze from me. "Don't be hard on yourself. I would have done the same. Emeline, are you well?"

"I'm fine, I think." She looks at the ground as she speaks. I want to wrap my arms around her. She's clearly trying to keep herself together and doing a good job of it. Blasted pirate. "Abner tried to fight him off before the pirate could tie him up, but the pirate thwarted him," she says.

Not what I would have expected from him.

"You're so brave," Jocelyn says as she brushes the dirt off Emeline's skirt. "I think I would have fainted on the spot. I should have stayed behind to help you set up camp. Then you wouldn't have had to face him alone."

Emeline pulls her lips into a thin straight line, then draws the corners up in a small smile and nods her head. She has to be raging on the inside. I can't help but be jealous. I hold myself together, but the harder things get, the more difficult it is.

Stewart breaks through my musings. "We won't be able to rest tonight. Let's pack up and get a move on. I don't want that cur to lead the rest of those pirates here, though I doubt he'll be able to return to the ship tonight. The further we are, the better I'll feel."

Constance dances into action, rushing the girls about the makeshift camp. Stewart goes to converse with Stephen and Brendan, while Robert steps closer to me. Abner glares at the two of us as if we may draw apart if he stares hard enough. Robert looks at him and jerks his head toward the supplies the elves brought. With a gruff snort, Abner shuffles over to the discarded packs.

Robert turns back to me. The world becomes unimportant—everything except Robert fades into the falling dusk. The bright moon lights half of his face as we lock gazes, and a current passes between us. The skin under his left eye is darkening, and a trickle of blood has dried from a gash on his forehead. My fingers itch to give it a healing touch and ease the pain.

"I'm glad to see you are well." His voice is like a soft caress.

"I'm good. You, though, look a little more worn out than the last time I saw you."

"Yes, well… the pirate wasn't too caring about where he shoved us, but it's of no importance. I feared he would follow you into town and manage to steal you away from Stewart. I'm set at ease to see you well, Adelei."

A warm blush creeps up my face. I glance to the side, hoping to hide it in the shadows and wishing it didn't come so easily around him.

He continues to look at me as he speaks. "Do you ever wish you spent more time with other humans?"

Before, all the time, but now they bring too much danger. "Not really. I think the race is interesting."

"I find that intriguing. Most humans avoid elves as much as possible. I have no qualms about being around them, but I am more comfortable around humans. Some elves have a different air about them, though I must say, I sense that same air when I'm around you."

I force a laugh, attempting to keep things light. "I've probably been around them too long, and some of their spells have worn off on me."

"Really? The difference I'm feeling is magic?"

"I believe so. Magic does leave a feeling around elves who cast spells, but most don't notice it. In fact, even those looking for it don't always feel it. Someone must be very focused to recognize it." I trail off, realizing what I said. The heat comes back, as I think of how much attention he must be paying to notice my spell. The fact that he detects other elves' magic is unusual but not rare. That he feels it in me makes me tingle with delight.

Silence drifts between us for a few moments. Robert runs his fingers through his hair and asks, "What do you know of their magic? Most humans are superstitious and frightened by it."

This time, my laugh comes hard and true, filling the air. Constance glances over at us, but I do my best to ignore her. "Elves don't have any power to be afraid of. In fact, most elves don't have much magic power anymore. Some say that long ago it used to be greater, and they had the ability to do many things. Now days, no elf is terribly powerful. All it does is enhance skills they already possess."

"Like what? Make their jokes funnier?"

I giggle. "No. For example, a healer. An elf already good at healing could use their magic to strengthen their ability. Or someone that's in tune with nature can control the weather, like the wind. A sailor like yourself could be good at that. If you were an elf you could use the wind to help you go faster or change the direction of the wind, though that could only be performed by a more accomplished elf."

"That would have been useful when our ship hit the storm that sent us to your island. Maybe we should hire an elf to help us when we reach Amara."

"It will be hard to find someone. Not only would you have to find a powerful elf—which is rare—you'd also have to find one willing to deal with the consequences of magic."

His forehead fills with wrinkles of confusion. "What type of consequences?"

"Well, spells don't come from thin air. They must use things that already exist. The change in those things is what brings about different effects. A healer draws from his own health or the health of another to help someone recover from a wound or illness. As a result, whoever's health is drawn from will be weaker. They won't have the wounds of the sick person, just the exhaustion. This is why Constance hasn't healed either of us. Speaking of her, have you noticed the meals not being quite as good as they were on the ship?"

"I have, though she still cooks better than most."

"She does. But it hasn't been as good because she doesn't want to use her magic on it. Magic brings out the flavor of the food, but the food loses some of its beneficial properties. Years ago, there was an elf who would use a high level of magic on everything she ate. Her body began to wither away, and no one could figure out why. The healers lost hope that she would live. It was when she was so ill she could no longer cook for herself that she started getting better. When she was well enough to cook and indulged too much with enhancing food, she got sick again. The healers eventually figured it out."

"It can be that deadly?"

Thinking of my own spell and the unknown consequences, I grow solemn. "Magic is not something to be taken lightly."

"I can imagine. This is a whole new concept to me, and I find it fascinating, not scary like many humans proclaim it is. What other consequences are there?"

"The wind we were speaking of before would change the weather. This reaction varies a lot since the weather itself is so unpredictable. It may range from inducing a blistering heat to pouring rain, sometimes even snow."

His voice becomes hushed. "Wait, does this mean that one of the elves traveling with us cast a spell on the wind to cause the pirates to fall behind before we made it to Port Varas?" His exclamation leaves a knot in my stomach. I chide myself for giving so much away and hope he doesn't figure out the correct answer. His puzzled expression clears, lighting his face. "I know. It was Constance."

I breathe a sigh of relief and shrug. "It may have been. She wouldn't be able to accompany you on your voyages, though. In fact, few elves would be willing to travel with humans, anyway. Humans are always antagonizing the elves."

"We humans do no more than the elves. They themselves bicker. I've heard many complaints about it through the years. The barrel incident is a perfect example of this."

"The barrel incident. That was nothing. I still remember how a merchant ship full of humans acted a few years ago in Amara. And the boar fiasco is not something elves will easily forget."

He chuckles and then sobers up. "Humans can't be judged from just that. Why don't elves understand it?"

I frown. "Maybe that's part of the problem. There's too much judging happening on both sides. Plus, there's no communication between races. I believe we are a lot more like humans than anyone realizes."

His forehead wrinkles. "We?"

I have to consider my words more carefully when around him. "Sorry. I guess I've spent too much time being with elves. I feel like I'm almost one of them."

His eyes twinkle merrily. "You certainly look pretty enough to be one of them."

"Robert, I already informed you I'm promised to another," I say, flustered though secretly pleased.

Straightening his back, Robert resumes the pose of a gentleman. "I'm sorry. That was inappropriate. Please forgive me. I wasn't thinking."

Our words don't match our actions, as we stay close enough to feel the other's breath.

Stewart speaks loudly to the side of us, breaking through Robert's hold on me. The two elves who have been accompanying us are with him. "These elves will be returning to town. They'll alert the guards that there has been a pirate about. Hopefully, there will be no trouble for them."

With the realization that everyone is staring at the two of us, my blush deepens, and I turn my face to the ground. Robert shifts toward the elves and moves to shake their hands in the human custom. Out of the corner of my eye, I see their foreheads wrinkle in confusion at the proffered hand, until Robert takes each of their hands in turn to shake them. "Thank you again, my good sirs," he says.

"Yes. Thank you." Stewart sounds distracted.

"Glad we could be of service," one of them says.

The two elves turn back in the direction they came and leave into the shadows of the night. Robert moves to help the group pick up camp, but I stand still, watching him.

Constance appears next to me, blocking my view. I try to keep myself from looking too guilty.

"Arabella," she whispers, "best be careful what you are thinking on. I saw the way the two of you were looking at each other, as did the rest of the group. You are to be married soon. This behavior won't be tolerated." Constance snaps back to the working group.

The reprimand stings as Constance goes back to the working group. My face flushes, but this time it's with guilt and anger instead of embarrassment. She's right. It doesn't seem to matter how many times I tell myself that, though. Robert still enters my thoughts. Worse yet, my reaction is a reflex, one not easily reined in. It would be best for me to avoid him the rest of the trip.

I scoff at myself. Like that's something I can do.

Just then, I realize Abner is looking at me with an ugly sneer. Camp is packed up, and I did nothing to help—again. That's probably what the look was for. His personality is much more suited to Captain Smythe's pirate ship than to Robert. How are the two of them friends?

The continued glare sends a shiver thought me. Abner is a perfect example of why elves and humans don't get along. He judged us from the moment he saw us, never allowing for a chance to get to know anyone. His anger is even directed at me, though he thinks I'm human.

Don't many elves have the same attitude toward humans, though? I should be more open-minded to having him in our group, instead of ignoring him outright. I head over to the others, trying to keep both things in mind.

Though only the moon and stars give out light, it's time to get moving toward Amara. I wince, thinking of my abused body. It will be four days—four long days—before we reach Amara. Exhaustion overwhelms me, but there is nothing to be done but walk. And walk. And walk. It doesn't matter. Soon, I'll be back to my life as a betrothed princess, and Robert will be out of my life.

Chapter
EIGHTEEN

༄

AS I CROSS into Amara, my feelings are a jumbled mess. I'm glad to be home, but uncertain about what waits for me there. The last four nights of travel remained uneventful. The forest changed to desert on the first night after the pirate's escape. We decided to sleep during the day and walk at night, so we could maintain a faster pace out of the heat. It was easier after getting some sleep and avoiding the heat, though my body still aches.

The nights, though pleasantly cool, were dull. My resolve to stay away from Robert didn't last. By the second night, I was ready to give in and talk to him. Unfortunately—or maybe fortunately—Constance's hawk-like gaze made any close proximity to Robert improbable, and the chances of talking to him were nil. We walked in the same group but as separated as we could be.

The bond between us is unaffected by the distance, and I am aware of his every move. The feelings pulsing through me are wonderful and frightening at the same time.

All through the second night, I kept fearing Captain Smythe would appear and thwart our journey home. Every noise would send me glancing, darting for danger. Jocelyn would do the same, most times grabbing on to me when she was startled. When we began walking on the third night, my fear lessened. The pirates wouldn't know the exact route we took and would be unable to follow us. Frustration replaced my fear of them. I've never been angry with Constance before, and it left me feeling guilty. I shouldn't be angry with her because she is just trying to help. I couldn't help myself, though.

By the time we set off the fourth night, my anger fled. I grew more morose with every step. Fatigue hit me full force, and each lift of my legs burned my muscles. My lungs didn't seem capable of holding enough oxygen to satisfy me. The only thing not tired or painful was the warming bond between me and Robert. It coursed through me, giving me energy to take each heavy step. I focused on it to pull me through the night as desert changed to forest again.

I sigh now, unsure if it is a happy sigh or a sad one. We are within sight of the castle, and I know our bond will soon be broken. It isn't something I want to happen, but since it must, it's best to get it over with.

When we leave the forest, we stand on a hill greeted by the west side of the castle, overlooking the city below. Seeing the castle that's been my home my entire life eases my heart a little.

The castle glows by the light of the countless torches' light on the foliage-laden paths leading to it. The outer walls are also lit by torches, and light shines through the curtained windows. The gray stones that make up the walls are covered with green ivy.

The main entrance is tall enough for four men standing on each other's shoulders and wide enough for their group to pass through, shoulders touching. The iron gate that covers the entrance glistens in the light. Seeing it unguarded brings a chill to my heart. There should be at least two guards on either side.

The castle looms over us as we walk closer. Four towers grace the front—two in the middle close to the entrance and one on each side. Knowing my bed lies in one of those towers makes me quicken my steps.

While we move across the front, I glance down the hill at the still-sleeping city below. A few lights twinkle through the vast city until it runs into the sea. The docks hold several large ships, but as far as I can tell, no elves are about at this hour. The briny sea smell wafts toward us and holds the comfort of home.

With my human form still donned and my cloak over my head, I follow our small group toward the servants' entrance of the castle, which I've never used before. We walk across the grassy plain to get there, my pulse jumping higher with each step. Only one person can fit through the entrance at a time. As we go through it and down the hall, I take note on how to get to my room. Constance leads us through several halls that all look the same, so I resort to counting them. As soon as we come across a servant, Constance bids him to follow.

"I need to tell the king and queen that you've been found," he whispers.

"We've had problems with coming home. I'll send you or someone for them shortly, but not until I'm certain the princess is secure," Constance replies.

"I'll follow you as long as it's quick."

"Fair enough."

We twist our way through the serpentine hallways to my suite and enter a concealed passage in the washroom. I move from there to my adjoined bedroom and smile at the familiar site. I can't help the wash of joy that comes over me and the tears that accompanies it. Never did I think I'd be so glad to see my room. The others lag behind as I hurry forward.

Next to me, a small closed door leads to my garment room. My bookshelf is still in the corner, overflowing. A round table is in front of it, with more books piled on top. I run my hands across them; I've missed the escape they offer. Across from us is a soft red chair and round table in front of an unlit fireplace.

The opposite wall is what really catches my attention. On both sides of the bed are tall, skinny windows, covered with deep red curtains. The enormous bed is in the middle, its four tall posts connected with a white drapery. The whispery cotton blankets beckon to me, begging me to dive into them and sleep for the next week, but the rest of the group slips in the room. No doubt Robert and Abner would think it odd if I curled up on a bed, in a room such as this.

Constance calls to the servant she asked to join us. "Will you please see these two gentlemen to a room? They will need to clean up and rest for the night before they leave. Quickly now, before the princess arrives. Stewart will inform the king and queen of our arrival."

"Yes, ma'am," he replies.

Stewart turns to Robert and Abner. "Thank you for coming with us. I don't know what would have happened to us without your presence. I'm sorry that you were hurt. A healer will be sent to you shortly. I'm only sorry we were unable to heal your wounds sooner."

"They aren't much, but we would appreciate it," Robert responds.

Abner jumps into the conversation, hostility edging his words. "Don't allow them to touch you. I know I won't let them use their black magic on me. You don't know what ill effects it will bring."

Robert spins on Abner, jaw clenching. "I'm very well aware of what comes with their magic. You best mind your tongue. When we left, you were warned that you had to respect these elves. That still holds now. They are trying to help. No harm will come upon us from them."

Abner's face flushes while he looks at the floor. He curls his fists into balls but says nothing further.

"I'm sorry for his behavior. I fear too many rumors have met his ears," Robert says.

"There's no need to apologize for him." Constance moves to him. She grabs a hold of both of his shoulders and pulls them in for a hug. What surprises me more is that tears are forming in her eyes. "We would have lost Adelei without you. I couldn't bear it if we did, and for that I thank you," she says.

Robert grasps both of her hands and kisses them. "The pleasure was all mine. Emeline. Jocelyn. Adelei." He looks at each of us in turn as he bids farewell.

His gaze lingers on me, but what can we possibly do about it? As much as I ache to throw myself in his arms and never leave their protection again, it simply can't be. It takes all the force of will I have left to keep from chasing after him when he leaves with Abner.

Stewart clears his throat, pulling my attention back to those still within my rooms. "My lady, if you wish to get cleaned up, I will inform the king and queen you have returned unharmed." He bows and leaves the room before I can reply.

"Finally." I give a sigh of relief. "I'm ready to be myself again."

I close my eyes. The tingling magic starts in my chest, moves to my head, and is followed by a stinging pain in my eyes, cheeks, and ears. I let out a cry and then a sigh and sit on one of the chairs by the bookcases. I lean my head against the chair's high back. Pure bliss. My limbs are heavy and limp. My mind goes mercifully blank. Until—that is—I realize how silent the room is.

I open my eyes to find Emeline, Jocelyn, and Constance staring at me, their expressions unreadable—except for Jocelyn's expression, which borders on shock. Unease pricks at me, making me sit up straighter. I've slouched before around them, so that shouldn't be it, but I straighten as best I can anyway. There's no sign of anything unusual when I check my clothes, save for the grime. It could be that they're appalled at seeing me on the clean chair in such a fashion, but I'm not sorry.

"What's wrong?" I ask.

Constance is the first to snap out of it. "Nothing of importance. We're all tired after our journey. It'll all be better after a goodnight's sleep. Let's get moving, so you can meet with your parents and get some rest."

I narrow my eyes at Jocelyn and Emeline, who are looking everywhere but at me. "Are you certain nothing is wrong?" I ask.

"Like I said, nothing of importance. We will worry about it later," Constance replies.

Maybe it is just dirty me on the clean chair or bruises from the fight with the pirate.

Constance continues. "Let's get you cleaned up. Girls, go put the rest of the bags away and come back here to help."

I watch the girls depart, feeling a pang of guilt at their having to work still after the strain we've all been under. Constance moves to the table next to me and places the only remaining bag on it beside some books. She unties the brown strings, and the bag falls open. She pulls out several articles of clothing, then gently pulls out the scroll I stumbled across.

"I'll be right back. I just want to get this in good hands before things get crazy."

That perks my curiosity. "Andries is here in Amara?"

"No, but I have a contact who'll know how to find him. Don't you worry about it, dear. Just rest."

I watch her leave the room, then can't help but slump back into the chair, closing my eyes again. This time, though, my mind doesn't stay blank. The expression on their faces makes my stomach twist in knots. Though it's been a while since we last ate, any appetite I had before is gone. The sick feeling creeps from my stomach to my throat.

Padding feet shuffle in the washroom, indicating Constance's return. The sound of water pouring into the bathtub calls to my filthy, aching body. Forcing the unease back down, I pull up out of the chair. My eyelids are heavy as I stumble over to the washroom. Constance stands by an almost full bathtub, ready for me. Jocelyn and Emeline return, laden with soaps, perfumes, and towels.

Once in, I insist the others get cleaned up. Constance refuses, but after a few feeble protests, Emeline and Jocelyn leave the way they came.

The warm water on my skin and the familiar perfume-scented water soothe my aching body. When the water grows cold, I get out and move to dress myself.

"My lady, let me help you with that." Emeline startles me. There was no noise when she entered. I was used to my servants coming and going without noise, but after being gone so long, it's almost like another world to be back here.

"You were quick to get ready," I say.

She gives me a timid smile. "I wanted to help you."

My heart warms, though she's still not looking at me. I'm making some headway with my more reserved servant. "I'm glad to have your help. Thank you," I say.

By the time I'm ready to face my parents, Jocelyn returns, looking refreshed. They all keep their gazes down since returning. Maybe it wasn't just me sitting on the chair.

We move to my personal sitting room. It's larger than my bedroom. The couch I sit on faces a wall with two doors on either side. Across from me are two chairs with a small refreshment table between them. A low, wooden walnut table is placed between the couch and chairs. Usually flowers or fruit are placed on the table, but now it's empty.

On the outside edges of the room are more chairs with little round seats and oval backs. A grand picture hangs on the west wall above the line of chairs, reflecting an exact duplicate picture that hangs on the east side of the room above a fireplace. Someone had lit a fire in anticipation of meeting with my parents here.

I don't know if my parents want me leaving my rooms if I'm supposed to be kidnapped. It's strange to think about what others must think is going on with me at this very moment. I watch the flames flicker and dance, casting strange patterns across the bricks surrounding them. After a few more minutes of my thoughts growing increasingly uneasy, a knock sounds.

Stewart enters. "My Lady Arabella, I present Their Royal Majesties King Sterling and Queen Pernilla, accompanied by Lord Octavian and his assistant Reginald."

The four enter formally, like they're being presented to a subject instead of a long lost heir to the throne. It's not unexpected, but the coldness leaves me wanting more than it ever has before. I sit stiff on my chair, trying not to give away my feelings.

Mother comes first, her slender white neck held straight, head high and proud. Her white face has been painted with crushed leaves and berries that make her cheeks rosy and lips a deep red. Her black hair is twisted into an elaborate knot on the back of her head. Something sparkly dances on the edges of her thinly pointed elven ear. I resist the urge to roll my eyes at her latest fashion and wonder how the sparkles were made.

Father steps in behind her, raking his dark-eyed gaze across the room until he finds me. His shoulders fall at the sight of me. He must be even more relieved to see me than I am him. His silver hair has been cut neat and trim since last time I saw him, leaving the tips of his ear visible. Though his face wouldn't be called handsome by elf standards, his thick lips and round nose give him a friendly appeal. One that's needed more than ever in this moment.

Octavian behind him drips with jewelry, and his plump body is draped with a rich green material. His right thumb idly twists a gold ring on his middle finger.

Looking more out of place among the royals, Reginald's tall, lanky frame is clothed in black. His olive skin is clear except for a thin white line above his right eyebrow. His dark hair is slicked back into a long ponytail instead of the usual unbound oily locks left to hang around his shoulders. He stumbles a little but recovers before anyone except me seems to notice.

Mother and Father take two chairs directly across from me, but Lord Octavian sits on the couch closer to me. Reginald stands behind Mother and Father, staring straight at me with a curious expression on his face.

Stewart shuts the door but stays in the room. No doubt there are guards stationed at each of the doors in the hallway. The process is a familiar one until my mother glances at me and shrieks.

"What has happened to your beautiful face?" She grimaces in horror.

Confused, I lift my hand to my cheek, wondering if I did something different to it. I didn't that I remember. I was too tired to bother with looking in the mirror after changing my face, but it feels as it should.

"Wha—what do you mean, Mother?"

"It's hideous."

Chapter
NINETEEN
❧

MY HEART SINKS, the sting of tears threatening. I take slow, deep breaths, trying to keep my response fitting a royal. Blinking rapidly, I'm able to push off the wild flow of emotion.

"Your Majesty, if you will permit me." Constance's tone doesn't leave it as a question. "Your daughter has shown a great display of magical powers. Not only that, but she has been wise in how she has chosen to use them. Did you know she was able to disguise herself as a human to evade capture by pirates?

Mother's horrified face melts into a wide-eyed and drop-jawed expression.

As Constance continues, her voice lowers. "After seeing the changes that have come over her face and hair, I would say we have found the consequences of the spell."

"Humph." Mother's upset word is tinged with anger, but still sound polished. "It was not worth it, then. That ugly thing does not look like my daughter."

Constance stands to her full height. "Well, she is, and a fine daughter at that."

"You have to admit it is an unusual change," Reginald interjects.

I shift my face down, trying to avoid the scrutiny of so many people. Why didn't anyone tell me? Why didn't I look in a mirror? Why did I believe that it could all be better in the morning?

"Unusual?" Mother points at me. "That is not unusual. It is unnatural."

"Forgive me, Your Highness," Stewart says. "I wish to convey to you how real the danger was. You daughter's ingenuity saved her the day the pirates came. Then, when we were almost overcome by pirates at sea, she cast a wind spell that pushed them away from us. She handled the threat of being kidnapped well, even when it was directed at her human form. Then she endured a taxing escape—something beyond her normal capability. Throughout it all, she never once complained, even when it became too much. When we were on our way, a pirate again tried to kidnap her. Though she was saved by the human, Robert, she sustained injuries. Not once did she complain about them."

Mother stops him with a wave of her hand. "Arabella should have known better. She shouldn't have needed help from…Robert? Who even is this Robert you speak of? Why was a human with you?"

"He's one of the men from the merchant ship that stopped on our island," Constance says. "If it wasn't for them, we wouldn't have been able to leave and come home. After the pirate ship attacked, Robert volunteered to escort us. He chose to help us of his own free will. Without his good nature, your daughter would be lost to us all."

"A human merchant is responsible for her being here?" Mother's perfectly arched eyebrows draw together in thought. I can't imagine what it is she could be thinking.

Reginald appears lost in thought as he speaks. "We should have a word with these humans."

"The humans are not important," Mother says. "It's not good enough to only save her life. Something should have been done to preserve her beauty."

Father cuts in. "Pernilla, she is still our daughter. This is nonsense. Forget it at once so we can move on to more important topics."

Never have I heard my father speak to my mother in such a tone before. Something about it has me sitting up straighter, though I still feel like cowering.

Mother shifts her angry gaze to him but says nothing further. Stewart and Constance move back to their posts, their gazes focused on me, filled with love and concern. I concentrate on my father, not wanting to deal with their pity.

His words would help stem the pain, but he said them in such a casual manner. He hasn't looked at me after the first initial glance.

Mother bursts into hysterical tears. I know my mother cares about beauty, but I didn't know to what lengths. I cringe.

Father pulls out a handkerchief from his pocket, hands it to her, and assesses her a minute before returning his attention to me. "I must say I'm rather worried." He stands and walks the room aimlessly.

Reginald speaks from his place behind the Queen. "We sent our best guard, as we planned."

"It went badly, though." Father paces faster. "After a day, we were surprised when a single guard returned. You see, when they weren't far out, an explosion destroyed the boat and killed all the guards save this one soul, though he was badly injured."

What ill news. I'm grateful to be sitting down, for there's no way my legs could hold me. Any thoughts of self-pity flee in that instance. All of those elves died. Some of them I even knew. My heart shatters. Who could have done such a thing?

I slump back in the chair, a stabbing pain through my chest. "How could this have happened?" I ask in a frightened whisper.

"We don't know for sure, my lady," Octavian replies. "We are speculating someone killed those elves so they couldn't protect you."

Father goes to stand by her, on the opposite side of Reginald, and places a hand on her shoulder. As soon as he touches her, she quiets her sobs, and dabs the handkerchief at her eyes.

Father speaks again. "The council has been trying to send you more help, but there isn't much left, and it was always delayed by some means. We have reason to believe someone within the castle is working against us."

"We've been so worried," Mother says, tears shining in her eyes but not clogging her voice. "We sent you out there, and you went, trusting us, but we couldn't even send you any help."

A sharp pain twists in my chest, tearing me apart.

Father takes on where Mother left off. "That is not all. Two days ago, we received a note, the contents of which were… well, disturbing, to say the least. Octavian, show Arabella the note."

Octavian stands and moves his bulk over to me. He kneels beside me and withdraws a folded parchment from somewhere within his cloak. He unfolds it and hands it to me.

While I read, my pulse becomes erratic.

King Sterling and Queen Pernilla,

We have kidnapped your daughter, Princess Arabella. We will be willing to return her, once you call off the wedding to the human. Blood can't be tainted by humans. You will follow our command to the letter as soon as you finish reading thi, if you ever wish to see your daughter alive again.

I gasp for air after reading the note a second time. I put my hand to my throat, trying to contain my emotions. The pirates tried to kidnap me, though they were unsuccessful. Yet the note was still delivered.

Octavian whispers, "They sent this note with a lock of your hair, my lady."

"A lock of my hair?" I place my hand on my head, feeling violated that someone managed to steal my hair without my knowing.

"We believed it to be true." Reginald comes to kneel beside Octavian. "We can only conclude the pirate must have had inside help who knew where you would be. They must have gotten rid of your guard, knowing you would be unprotected. They didn't think you'd be a problem to capture. But you, my lady, very cleverly outwitted them."

He is the only person who has truly looked at me since I let go of my spell. I try to control the shiver that comes, but there's no way to repress it. He leans in closer, inspecting my face.

Octavian takes my hand, turning my attention to him when I'd much rather ignore them both. Better yet, knock them both on the side of the head with the hilt of my sword. Just because things are different doesn't give them a right to invade my space.

"Whoever is helping them in this castle," Octavian says, "must have sent the note, thinking you were captured yet that was not the case."

"There is one other problem." My father's hesitant voice takes on an unusual tone. "Since we believed this note to be true, we dared not risk your life. As soon as we read and discussed the note, we sent an emissary to King and Queen Leland with a letter telling them we are withdrawing your betrothal. I fear it will lead to war, but we couldn't risk your safety."

My whole body feels limp, almost like it's someone else's. Standing, I brush past the two councilors and walk over to the glowing fireplace. My mind is completely numb from the news I have always desired to hear. Now that I've heard it, I feel odd. Somehow after everything, this isn't what I want to hear anymore. At least I don't think it is?

I brush any thought of the betrothal aside and try to focus on the more immediate problem. "Who can we trust? If they have help from the inside, there's no one. I know those who went with me are trustworthy. None of them could have set this plot because they would have just handed me over. At least we can trust them."

My father walks over to me, his gaze still avoiding my face. "You let us worry about those things. For now, go get some rest. The whole country thinks you have been kidnapped, and we must announce that you have been found. Get some rest, and then we shall have a feast in celebration of your safe return."

Father, Octavian, Reginald, and Stewart all leave the room, but my mother remains. She sits, watching her hands twist the dampened handkerchief and saying nothing. Her eyes look like they might soon turn into another waterfall. Though she's obviously troubled, she still manages to look elegant and graceful.

"Arabella, I'm sorry for all we have put you through. No longer having your beauty is a terrible loss." Mother continues to speak, sounding almost as if she's talking to herself. "The satin brown hair was her best attribute, too. Now it's a scraggly looking mess. And the loss of her beautiful blue eyes and creamy skin, both now marred. The leaf-like ears make me sick. I don't even want to think of them anymore. It will all give me nightmares."

I clamp my jaw shut and hold in the torrent raging inside me. My eyes and nose sting. Taking a deep breath, I manage to say, "Then let us not think of it, mother. Did you wish to speak to me of something else?"

Mother sniffs and glances at the fire. "Yes. You don't want to think of what has happened anymore. I will think of some way to fix this for you."

Grinding my teeth, I just nod. I keep my tear filled eyes on my skirt while Mother continues.

"I know that you have always resented your betrothal. Your father and I did what we thought was right at the time. Well, that is no longer, and Lord Octavian has asked for your hand. Your father and I have discussed it, and we feel this would be best, though I don't know if he will take you after this new development."

Stunned, I can do nothing more than stare at mother with wide eyes. Finally, I move over to a chair and plop into it. This is what I wanted for so long. I am no longer required to marry the human prince, but that freedom is marred by Lord Octavian. A cold chill runs across me just thinking on it.

"My dear Arabella, we are so glad to know you are safe." Mother lifts her chin. "I'll leave you alone now so you can rest."

With that said, she flees the room. Constance tries to come near me, but there's too much pain to have her or anyone else around. I dismiss all my servants with a wave of my hand and meander into my room.

I slip off the uncomfortable shoes and fall onto the bed. The soft feather bed eases my aching back but don't give as much comfort as I thought.

I cry into my pillow, unable to stem the flow of pain. All those elves lost their lives because of me. How can I live with that thought? Especially if my broken betrothal will create a war. For a long, long while, nothing else consumes my thoughts. The sobs eventually ebb. My muscles ease, though I still can't relax.

My dream has come true. The betrothal is gone, but look at the price that has already been paid, with more to come. I sigh and roll over, trying to get more comfortable. I work to stifle anymore crying. There's been enough of that for now.

If I had been allowed to choose my own husband, maybe things wouldn't look quite as dire, but Octavian? What are my parents thinking? Don't they know me better than that? I suppose not. My mother has always been superficial, but I didn't realize she would loathe me just for the loss of my beauty.

"I must look repulsive." Fresh tears course through me when I realize I don't dare look in a mirror.

Chapter
TWENTY

༄

WAKE UP, MY LADY," Jocelyn's voice gently calls
to me. "It's time for you to get ready for the feast."
I don't remember falling asleep. I just remember the whirlwind of emotions and thought streaming out of
me, leaving me exhausted. The tears leave my eyelids swollen,
making it even harder to open them. Blinking a few times, I
give up and close them again. I roll over, pulling the covers
over my pounding head.

Emeline's voice sounds through the layers of fabric. "The
Queen wants you ready and said she wanted you to start now."

The sobs from last night threaten to overwhelm me again. I
wish to bury my head in the mess of pillows instead of coming
out to face the royal court. Taking several deep breaths, I roll
out of bed.

The beautiful gown I'd dressed in earlier is wrinkled
beyond quick repair. Any magic used to get the wrinkles out

would leave the fabric more faded and in even worse-looking shape than it already was. I'd been hoping I could have just worn it and not play dress up again. That is no longer an option, but Jocelyn has already assessed the situation.

"I hope it's all right, My Lady. I took the liberty of picking a dress for you. This one looked good, though I was unsure of what you'd want to wear tonight. If there's something else you'd like better, I'd be happy to get it for you."

"It is perfect," I tell her while Emeline holds up the simple, yet elegant blue dress up for me to see. Though in all truth, I have a hard time pretending to care which dress it is.

Jocelyn runs into the bathroom to find some adornments to match for my hair. Emeline sets the dress down and moves to help her prepare. Both girls avoid looking directly at me. My hands twist in the folds of my dress. If they can't look at me, how will the nobles react to me at the feast?

Jocelyn returns, and both maids help me into the blue satin gown. When they finish, I take a deep breath, preparing to see myself for the first time in days. Though I know it won't happen, I still hope to see my familiar elven form. With one last push, I look in the mirror.

The eyes staring back at me are brown around the irises and have the blue that used to dominate tinting the edges. My hair is pulled up in an intricate pattern with small white flowers weaved through instead of my usual crown. An attempt to hide the dirty blond no doubt. My old, dark brown hair would have made a better contrast.

I brush aside the hair covering the tips of my ears. They are no longer sharply pointed like an elf's, but neither are they rounded like a humans. Letting the hair back down, I run my hand over my lightly freckled cheek. I miss my creamy complexion, vain though it may be.

Moving my hand back to my side, I take in the upturned nose and mouth that remained the same. Though I look neither like my elven or human form, I take comfort in the familiarity that remains. It isn't so bad. Mother had exaggerated as usual. I turned away from the mirror.

Emeline and Jocelyn applied make-up to my face, something they had never done before. The crushed herbs tickle my nose and leave my face heavy. With a few more minor adjustments left, Constance appears.

"Jocelyn. Emeline. You both have done a fine job. You are both dismissed, free to do what you will this evening. I will finish here and help the Princess when she retires for the evening."

A smile grows on Jocelyn's face. "Thank you, Constance. It'll be nice having some time off. Where shall I start?" She mutters to herself as she leaves the room. Emeline gives a little wave then follows after with a grin on her face.

After they leave the room, Constance makes a few minor adjustments, remaining quiet. The tension coming from her is palpable as she rearranges some hairpins. Shifting uneasily in my seat, I turn to face her.

"Please tell me what's bothering you."

"My dear child." She stops her work and sits down in a chair close to me. "No matter what your mother says, you are still beautiful. Your mother places too much importance on physical things. Looks, clothes, and objects mean more to her than they should. She has ordered me to help you to come back to your original self. While I won't stop you if that is what you wish, I can't condone the action. Even if you try, who knows what the results would be. Magic can be a fickle thing, and I fear it could go worse, not better. I will support you in whatever you decide."

"But why do you not just follow my mother's orders? She'll be very cross with you when she finds out. Maybe I should try just so she doesn't know of your disobedience."

"No, my dear. Don't worry about her actions toward me. I can take care of myself. If you truly wish to try, go ahead, but only if it is what you want. Please don't do so just for your mother."

I nod, looking at the floor. When I don't speak, Constance continues, "Yes, well, you needn't decide now. Plenty of time for that."

Constance stands and puts the finishing touches on my hair. While she finishes, I think on her words. I close my eyes, and after a time, reopen them to look in the nearby mirror. It is true my face doesn't hold the same former beauty, but I just can't find it as hideous as Mother does. It's a change I think I can grow accustomed to.

"Finished, my dear," Constance says. "Go and enjoy your meal."

"Thank you." I stroll out of the room, fingers twisting in my skirt.

THE FOOD LOOKS divine, but tastes dry and flavorless. Everyone around me is laughing and talking. I'm sitting as far from the main table as possible, in a corner. Occasionally, a noble peers around the piles of food to look at me and grimace. I force myself to always smile back.

The longer the night goes on, the smaller the piles of food get and the more people can see me. Everyone wears fine clothing of varying colors and styles, though the more detailed clothing like what my mother is wearing is most prevalent.

The grand hall holds three long tables around the edges of the room. Elves start gathering in the middle of the room for dancing. My parents laugh and chat with people around them until my father ushers my mother to the middle of the room. Music starts up, and they dance. Once they begin, others follow suit. After the first song ends, another starts, but my parents return to their place at the center table.

When enough time passes that I can leave without causing a commotion, I escape to the deserted balcony. Looking up at the stars, I attempt to ignore the faint chatter and music coming from the dining hall.

"Princess, I have been waiting for a chance to talk to you all night." Reginald interrupts my solitude and makes me jump. A chill runs up my spine as I turn to him. I've never cared much for him, but my parents and Octavian cherish his advice. Pulling out my most congenial self, I smile but remain silent.

"What was it like? Changing your face, I mean," he says.

My smile falters. "It hurt."

"Interesting." Reginald rubs his smooth chin. "What gave you the idea to change it?"

I choose my words carefully. "If you don't mind, I'd prefer not to speak of it."

Octavian appears behind Reginald with a scowl. "I think it would be best if you left now, Reginald."

"Yes. Of course." Reginald bows to me. "Forgive me. It wasn't my intention to offend." He nods to Octavian as he leaves.

Octavian's scowl fades with his assistant. "Please forgive him. He's a tremendous help but still has much to learn."

"Don't concern yourself over it." I wave him off. My thoughts shift to his proposal of marriage. I shiver and work to rid the balcony of him as soon as I can. "What can I do for you this evening?"

"I'd like to have a word with you."

It doesn't sound like I can get rid of him easily, then. "What is it you wish to converse?"

"You." A smile creeps up on his face, but his beady eyes look everywhere but at my face. "I've watched you these last few years. You've become a fine woman. I can live with your changed face. I hope to marry you soon."

"I'm certain you do." I try not let sarcasm lace my words. He is old enough to be my father. Of course, he'd be anxious to get married. It won't be to me, though.

I turn back to the railing, look out to the dark but still beautiful garden below, and try not to vomit in it. He disgusts me. At least I don't have to endure his leers since my face took on a new form. An unexpectedly good consequence.

"Marriage to a fine elf, such as myself, will help open your eyes to the way things could be done. Help you make decisions. You will accomplish much with me at your side. It's time for things to change around here."

I agree that things need to be different, but I don't believe we hold the same feelings on what changes should be made. He moves closer, his breath on my neck sending tingles of discomfort through my body. I move to a chair facing him but drape my legs out in front of me in an unladylike fashion to keep distance between us.

I evaluate him during the silence as he stands with his brows drawn together. Gaudy jewelry adorns most of his fingers and neck. His clothes are of the latest fashion, tailor-made to fit his bulky form. He cares for things of status, not for me. It is apparent from looking at him that he's too much like my mother.

"I do agree things can't stay so close to war with humans," I say. "We shall soon topple if we don't resolve our differences."

"Yes, yes." He flips his jeweled hand. "But when we're married, you can let me worry about such difficulties while you attend to more womanly matters."

"Thank you for the offer." Anger surges through me, but I have to be cautious as he's a member of the court. "I feel, though, that this business with Prince Phillip is a big misunderstanding. If we explain things to the humans, maybe the betrothal can be pieced back together, and we can work on repairing the rift between us."

I try to keep a smile on, but his eyes grow dark. Spiteful. For the first time, he looks directly at my face. He moves the bulk of his body toward me. He raises his hand, and I think he's going to strike me. Instead he brings it down slowly to my cheek. His touch sends my body feeling achy and sick.

"We shall see." His voice is venomous.

He storms off the balcony. I thought things couldn't be worse, but this is. Much worse. It's time for the feast to end, at least for me.

The gazes of the gathered nobles follow me when I reenter. I ignore them, concentrating on my parents seated at the head of the grand table. My hand tingles within the folds of my dress. I stop behind them, and my father turns to look at me. Mother stays facing forward, though conversation has stopped around her.

"Good night, Father. Mother." I curtsy.

"Good night, Arabella."

My heart flickers with a hope I've only found with Constance when my father looks directly at me. That hope is dashed when my mother won't glance in my direction.

I turn and flee the room as fast as I can within the social norms. I wind my way through the empty halls, heading for my sanctuary. My feet pad on the thick rugs. The stone walls on the way to my room are covered with tapestries of my ancestors. I stop to look at one that hangs at the end of the hall. Ancient artwork, probably one of the oldest in the castle.

"What would you do if you were in my position?" I ask the painting. "I doubt you worried about anything for your face looks so serene."

I turn down the adjoining hall and enter my suite several doors down. I shut the door behind me and lean against it in the dark. A headache is knotting itself in my head. I try to rub it away. I loath that I'm considering calling my betrothal back on. I became free of it only to desperately want it back.

I might as well try to do what is best for the people. My people. My stomach churns at the thought.

I move into the bedroom, running into a chair on my way. The low fire gives a soft glow to the corner of my room. Constance isn't here, likely thinking I'll be at the feast for some time. With difficulty and much reaching, I manage to change out of my dress and carefully drape it across the chair. I slip into my white cotton nightgown and pull my hair down. I look at my bed, longing for sleep, but I know it's going to be a long, restless night.

Chapter
TWENTY-ONE

CONSTANCE CAME IN earlier to check on me but left after she saw I took care of everything. Since then, sleep is more fitful. Giving way to the noise within my head, I slip out of bed, grab my white robe, and wrap it tightly around me. I shudder as the cool silk embraces my skin.

My room is dark, save for a little moonlight streaming in through the window. As I head toward it, there's a noise in the sitting room. After the events of the last few weeks, knots twist up in my chest. None of the maids would come through the sitting room, and no one else would come this time of night. I head toward the washroom, where the servants' entrance is, so I can hide.

I'm probably being silly. After all, there are guards outside my door, and I'm at home, but I go nevertheless. As I make it into the washroom, there's the soft thud of footsteps in my bedroom. It sounds like they move toward my bed. I glance around the corner, trying to see while remaining out of sight.

A large dark figure is surrounded by moonlight. This is not one of my servants, though the burly man looks familiar. An urgent sense to leave grabs hold of me and yanks me backward.

I head to the servants' entrance. On the way out of the dark room, I hit something and send it crashing to the floor. My breath catches in my throat.

"Ahh!" Captain Smythe's voice rings out from the other room, sending a piercing chill down my spine. "Come here, Princess. I won't hurt you."

Fear grips my chest. I slide behind the tapestry covering the servants' entrance and try to move silently. Hearing him enter the washroom, I run down the dimly lit passage, following the unfamiliar path that leads outside as best as I can. Finding help through the twist of hallways is improbabl since I don't know where they all lead. I could very well wind up lost in a deserted part of the castle.

Stepping lightly, I continue through the maze of hallways, the echoes of footsteps fading behind me. Either he is falling behind or being very quiet. My guess is for the latter. The thought sends my body into flight mood. I try to calm my breathing as I continue forward, getting rid of as much noise as I can.

Turning the last bend, I pull up the hood of my robe and decide to put on my magical disguise, hoping it will help if he—magic forbid—catches up to me. My life is more important than any beauty I might lose. I could play innocent about the princess, though he may take Adelei, too.

My pulse pounds in my ears. Frantic thoughts race through me. I have to get away. The forest is closer than the front entrance. If I can make it there, I might lose him.

The problem is my white robe will be easy to see against the inky night. I glance behind me to see if Captain Smythe is chasing me out of the castle.

Thud.

I fall against a heavy mass. Strong arms wrap around me as I struggle to get free. My throat is closing up. Body screaming for freedom. A familiar scent fills my nose, urging me to calm down. A comforting, masculine scent.

Fear still grips me, moving my defensive training into action. I muster all my strength and run off. I pump my legs as fast and hard as I can until a groan reaches me, and I hesitate.

I look back to find Robert, holding his stomach. I should have recognized his scent sooner. Though, with whom I'm running from, I know why it didn't register.

Robert groans again. "Adelei."

"Robert." I rush back toward him. "Captain Smythe is chasing me."

He lifts an eyebrow at me, his face pain ridden. His lips move as if he's about to speak when someone grabs me from behind, wrapping hefty fingers around my mouth. I try to scream anyway.

Robert punches the man's face a foot or so above me. The man calls out and lets me go. I stumble to the grass but roll back to my feet.

I run up the hill toward the thin woods we had journeyed through to get to Amara. The thunk of two bodies hitting together sounds through the air. I chance glancing back to see Robert leaning over Captain Smythe. A dark liquid gushes from Captain Smythe's nose onto his shirt. He's moving on the ground, sword in hand.

I turn all the way toward them, trying to think of a way to help. Robert gives a fierce blow to Captain Smythe's stomach, kicks the sword out of his hand, and takes off running. He motions me forward, toward the forest.

Feet pound on uneven terrain that cuts into my bare soles. I ignore the pain and press on. We run and run. There's no sign of being followed, yet we keep going. Finally the sharp ache in my side becomes too much. I slow, and Robert follows suit.

I'm gasping for breath. Robert isn't much better as he says, "I think we lost him." He places a comforting hand at the small of my back. "I'm sorry you had to see that. I don't normally kick a man when he's down, but I feared he'd be too quick to follow."

"I understand," I say between puffs of air. "Thank you for your help."

"What's going on?"

"Let's continue walking, and I'll tell you. I don't wish for him to catch up with us."

He nods in agreement, and we walk toward the beach. The rush of the moment catches up with me, and my cheeks burn. I've been lying too long. "You know that the princess has been in danger." He nods, and I go on. "I was placed in her room as a decoy in case anything happened. I don't look like her, but at least someone would be in her place in case anyone was watching. I admit that I, too, couldn't sleep."

Gazing upon him, just being with him, stirs up all my feelings even more than when I'm not with him. No wonder I couldn't sleep. "I had just gotten up and was about the pace around the room when I heard a noise in the sitting room. Frightened, I hid in the washroom and headed out the servants' entrance. In my haste to leave, I knocked something over and Captain Smythe spoke. Eventually, I made it out of the castle where I bumped into you."

He looks at me thoughtfully. I pull his jacket round me tighter.

"Tell me one thing. Why do they need a decoy? Why not place extra guards around her?"

"Well, uh… I suppose they wanted extra protection. There should have been someone standing guard outside the door, which has me worried for whoever that was supposed to be. They think someone on the inside is working against us, which may explain a lot. Plus, the attempted kidnapping frightened the king and queen into taking extra precautions. The cancellation of her betrothal also worri—"

Robert's well-defined jaw drops, his face pales, and his eyes grow large. I place a hand on his arm. He relaxes a little under my touch, coming to look more like himself, but still in a state of shock.

"Have you not heard the news? I thought someone would have told you after we returned," I say. He shakes his head, so I continue. "The king and queen decided to call off the wedding despite the serious consequences because of the ransom note they received. Thinking the pirates actually had m—the princess when they received it, they weren't willing to wager on her life."

He sits on a rock, and I stand next to him, wondering what he is thinking. He rubs his eyes and then the back of his neck. Maybe I'm right to want to restore the betrothal. He seems so upset by the news. If he cares so much, maybe others do as well.

I stiffen my back while I consider my other option. The human prince can't possibly be as bad as Octavian. Can he?

After several moments of silence, Robert regains his composure. "I'm sorry. This news is such a surprise. I've never been one to agree with arranged betrothals, but I know what this will do to my people."

"Your people? I like to think of us all being the same. Equal, whether we belong to the same race or not. Really, the biggest difference between humans and elves is magic and outward appearance." My tone grows angrier with each word.

Frustrated, I storm off in the direction I hear the ocean waves crashing in. Robert catches up when the sandy beach meets the hardened wooden floor.

"Adelei, I'm sorry. He gently pulls me to a stop. He wraps both arms around me. "I didn't mean it that way at all. I believe humans and elves are not all that different, but I know many feel they are. This marriage would have been a good thing for both races."

His words enter my thoughts and make sense, but they barely register. The feel of his arms around me is distracting. I lay my head on his chest and breathe in his scent. The rhythmic movement of his chest soothes me. The warm, tingling sensation flickers within me, and then flames outward to the rest of my body. I look up at him, my lips aching to find his.

Betrothed.

The single-word thought stiffens my body. Heart feeling like it's falling apart, ripping into tiny little pieces, and being stomped on, I push away from his warmth. Tears prick at my eyes, but I refuse to let them fall even when I turn my back to him.

"I wouldn't worry about it too much," I say. "I know the princess wants to make amends with the humans. She won't tolerate something that will lead to war, especially not because of her, even if many would have her keep it broken off."

I glance up at him, the unshed tears filling my eyes. His expression ranges through a multitude of emotions I wish to enjoy the time I have left with him, but I can't. The sound of the sea beckons me, asking me to wait just a little longer.

"Come. Let us walk by the sea, and then we will return to the castle. Captain Smythe hopefully will be searching elsewhere by then."

Robert nods his agreement and follows me the short distance to the beach. As the trees finish clearing, I look out onto the sea with longing. My heart urges me to leave with Robert and never come back.

Of course, he doesn't even know who I am. I don't even really know who he is. Just that we have a connection. And that connection is one I so desperately want to explore. The first step onto the sand is a soothing change.

"Adelei, stop." Robert's voice is quiet, but full of warning.

I halt, being pulled out of my wistful thoughts and look around. A ways down the beach is a row boat. A ship is anchored behind it in the water, and though no sails are unfurled, a warning fills my chest.

Robert motions back toward the castle, and I trail after him. Looking back one last time, I stop.

"Wait. I think I see two people," I whisper.

"No, Adelei. It's too dangerous."

I know I should heed the warning, but we need more information. I silently creep forward, remaining hidden in the foliage. Both of the figures look familiar, but I need a closer look to know who they are. Worry fills my chest.

Hoping my eyes are deceiving me, I squint trying to get a better view. The voice carried by the wind rises, making the words almost distinguishable. Captain Smythe. He is one of the men, of that there is no doubt. All of me goes cold just thinking it. His mammoth body is easy to spot even with only the faint moonlight.

The two were talking. I struggle to hear over the crashing waves. Even though I thought they might be at the beach, seeing them here is something else entirely.

I struggle to hear the conversation over the crashing waves. To give meaning to their words. The second man is hiding from the milky moonlight, in the shadows. Captain Smythe storms away from the trees, and the man in the shadows moves out, his huge figure coming into view.

Chapter
TWENTY-TWO

HOW COULD YOU lose her again?" Octavian's voice fills the air with rage as it drifts to us. "You were supposed to kidnap her, and you couldn't. Tonight I give her directly to you, and you return with only a bloody, broken nose. You're supposed to be the most fearsome pirate."

Captain Smythe's temper looks like it's on the verge of boiling over. His fists are clenched, his body shaking, but his face is hardened with resolve, and he gains his composure.

All the while, Octavian stares him down, eyes bulging out of his head.

When Captain Smythe speaks, the words are loud and surprisingly clear. "Tonight, I went myself, to make sure the job was done. You said she'd be easy to get once the guard was taken care of. Too bad she was already on her way out. You also said she'd be on Sulamay Island with no guards. You were right about the guards, but she was gone too."

Robert places his hand on my shoulder and pulls at me, eager to leave. Yet we both stay and listen while the drama continues to unfold, intrigue pulling us in. I scoot closer to him, warmth comforting my otherwise rigid body.

"Your excuses are worthless. I told you to leave the castle intact and not hurt anyone. All you had to do was grab the princess and leave. This is going to be my castle. *My* things. And you stole my tapestries. You turned an easy job and easy money into a catastrophe that will get you little." Octavian's voice quivers with anger. "You will go find the princess and bring her to me now."

"Your misinformation has done nothing but add danger for me and my men. I must insist that I get the human servant, Adelei, on top of my full pay, upon the princess's delivery."

Robert's hold on me tightens, and he moves between me and the two men, though they are still unaware of our presence. I want to laugh, and would, if it wasn't for the gravity of the situation and the fact that it would give us away.

"Full pay is out of the question. And what are you talking about, you stupid pirate?" Octavian sneers. "Who is Adelei?"

"She is Princess Arabella's servant. A human girl more beautiful than any I have ever met. I will be taking her with me if you want the job done."

"You bumbling idiot. The Princess has no servant by the name of *Adelei*. The only human servant she has is Jocelyn, though you can have her if you wish."

My throat constricts.

"No one calls me an idiot. I met her and saw her with my own eyes. You won't pretend she doesn't exist and secret her away for yourself. I will have Adelei. She was one of the servants at the castle, and I know they have returned. You will give her to me with all of my pay, or you can start doing the dirty work yourself."

Octavian slapped his jeweled fist into the captain's shoulder and with a venomous voice says, "You fool. Adelei must be Princess Arabella. That's why she has turned into a homely creature. Go find her, whatever she looks like, and I will double your pay. But you won't be taking her with you. And do not threaten me again, filthy scum."

My hand flies to my throat, and my mouth goes dry. I glance at Robert, wondering what he may think of the news. He is staring at me with wide, disbelieving eyes. I hate myself for not being able to tell him the truth. I wish I told him as soon as we arrived at the castle.

Whatever my feelings, it won't be long before Captain Smythe and Octavian find me if we don't get somewhere safe. With my secret identity revealed, my only recourse is finding a well-protected hiding spot. What I was supposed to have in the first place. I need to return to the castle and tell my parents the identity of the insider. They will be distraught over the news.

Robert whispers in my ear, his voice a state of awe, jolting me out of my trance.

"Adelei, is this true? You are the princess? I can't believe this. How can you be?" Robert whispers in my ear, his voice full awe, jolting me out of my trance.

I wince. "I'm sorry about the lies. It was necessary."

Robert runs his hand through his hair. "I just can't believe it. You—"

Before he can finish, I realize the captain and Octavian are headed for us. I motion to Robert, who nods with understanding. We edge back deeper into the forest, and I feel the ground with my bare feet. Octavian and Captain Smythe stop to argue again right next to where we were a few moments ago. I don't bother to listen to the new quibble.

Once we are out of ear shot, Robert and I run to the castle.

"Adelei—I mean Princess Arabella," he says between huffs of breath, "you said you were promised to another, but to Prince Phillip?"

"We'll talk later," I puff out and open the entrance that we arrived at. "I need to warn my parents. Lord Octavian is one of their most trusted advisers. My father, he gave permission for Octavian to marry me. He won't be far behind. We must tell them before they do something even more dimwitted."

I slip through the door, and Robert follows after. Navigating the hallways, I head toward my room. I let the magic spell fizzle with a cry, revealing my new face.

I open the door leading into my washroom. A bright light and worried voices greet me. We both step into the bathroom and then out into my room. My parents and personal servants stand conversing, their faces scrunched together in worry. When they register my presence, the frantic conversations cease.

"Arabella, we thought something terrible happened," Constance calls to me as she runs to greet me. Lovingly, she wraps her arms around me for the first time ever. "Where did this jacket come from? How did this blood get on your robe? Are you hurt?"

Constance checks every inch of me, looking for the wound.

"My Lady, I've been so worried about you. I'm so relieved to see you are well." Jocelyn looks like she wants to say more, but after eying the King and Queen, says nothing else. Emeline stands next to her, brows drawn together.

My mother speaks, drawing everyone's awareness to Robert. "Who are you?"

He's staring at me so intently I don't think he even heard the question.

"Constance, everyone, I'm fine. If you give me a moment to explain. It's very important." I turn toward my mother. "This is Robert. He saved me from Captain Smythe just now. He was the one that escorted us from Port Varas."

Mother's eyes jut out at Robert. "This common sailor has no business being with you."

He holds her gaze, jaw clenching.

"Your Majesty, now isn't the time for this discussion," Constance says firmly.

Mother's eyes narrow. "Mind your place, Constance."

I interrupt in an attempt to divert my mother's attention. "Why are you all gathered in my room?"

Mother doesn't take her gaze from Constance, but Constance replies, calm as ever, "A servant found Stewart unconscious in the hallway. Someone hit him hard, but he should be fine. We were all distraught and trying to figure out what should be done when you came. What happened?"

I glance at Stewart with concern. It dawns on me he's sitting in a chair when he always stands, a damp cloth on his head. Even though he's pale and looks miserable, he smiles at me. Feeling at least a little better, I rehearse my tale.

"Captain Smythe came in here trying to find me. Luckily, I was already awake and heard him enter. I escaped through the servants' entrance, and he followed me outside. I ran into Robert and asked for his help when the Captain skulked up from behind and grabbed me. Robert was kind enough to break his nose, but I fear the blood will not come out of my robe."

Constance shakes her head, but doesn't interrupt the narrative.

"We ran through the woods, coming out by the sea, making sure that we were not followed. We were about to return when we noticed a ship anchored in the bay. I was drawn to it, so I got a closer look. It was Captain Smythe's ship. He was standing on the beach not far off, conversing with Octavian."

My parents' expressions fall slack. My mother sways, and my father gently helps her get to a chair while I continue.

"It was him all along. He must have used his charm to convince you both to have me sent to the island so no one would know where I was. I remember now that it was his idea to begin with. He must have had the guard killed so they could not be there to protect me when his pirate friend came. I do not know what madness has consumed him, but something must be done quickly."

The room remains silent for several moments as everyone digests the news. Betrayal at the highest level permeates the air around us. The King shifts his weight uncomfortably from one foot to the other.

"Well, Arabella," my father says. "Let's get you somewhere that's actually safe while we deal with Lord Octavian. It won't be an easy task, but it must be done. I don't want you near while we are dealing with him."

"I can take her to the servants' quarters," Emeline offers. "He wouldn't think to look for her there."

"That should work," my father says. "First, Arabella, why don't you go ahead and get changed and cleaned up? Do it quickly, though."

Constance opens the door and ushers the men into the sitting room, including Robert. She and Jocelyn help me clean up while Emeline fetches some new clothes. Constance takes the dress from Emeline and helps me put it on. My mother sits in a chair by the fireplace, watching the women hurry about. While we work, I listen to the conversation taking place in the sitting room.

"Your Majesty, I agree. Something must be done about these pirates as well. They are anchored too close to Amara. It will be a fierce battle unless something is done to stop them."

"Yes. Most of my men are still out looking for Arabella, and the best of them were killed by Lord Octavian's treachery. It will be a while before we can get enough men gathered together to battle against them. They may even slip through our fingers before anything can be done."

"If I may be permitted, your Majesty, our merchant vessel is well-trained. With all the pirates that roam the sea, we have worked hard to magnify our fighting skills. I would be honored to go to the Captain of our vessel and ask for our assistance on your behalf. We can hold them where they are until your men can be gathered. Then, if some of them need to help you search for and detain Octavian, you will not be spread so thin."

"Yes, I think this is a fine plan. I honestly do not want to accept your help, but there is no other choice if we are to stop them. I will not have you do all this work without—"

"Jocelyn, you will go with Emeline to help," Constance says, pulling me from the conversation in the other room. I nod, thank Constance, and leave out the servants' entrance without a word from my mother, who is still sulking in a corner. Emeline leads the way with me following and Jocelyn coming up from behind.

"You both stay here," Emeline says when we reach the entrance to the servants' quarters. "I will check that it's safe."

Feeling jittery, I wait in the small dimly lit hallway with Jocelyn. The hairs on the back of my neck rise more with each passing second. Jocelyn places her hand on mine and gives me a warming smile. Returning the smile, I try not to worry. Against my will, my hand knots in the folds of my dress.

"Someone has been looking for you," Emeline says on her return, eyes wide. "I was mistaken about this place, but I know an empty guest room where we could go that will be safe."

"Maybe we should go back," Jocelyn says. "Then we can let those we trust protect her, or at least tell them where we will be. I don't like that someone has already been down here to check on her. We don't even know who they are. Why would they have come here? Are they trying to help or not? I can even go back by myself if you want. It may help us know what to do."

"No. We were told to take her some place safe, and so we shall. You can tell them where we are once you see the room I have in mind."

Not wanting to add tension between the two girls, I remain silent. It's been a long night already and I'm in no mood to argue. Plus, the closer I become to them, the more I loathe ordering them about. If I do speak, they'll have to follow my words.

"That should work," Jocelyn says. "Lead the way."

Emeline leads us back through the passages, twisting and turning. After a long walk, Emeline finally comes to a door. Instead of checking this one out to see if it is safe, she walks right in. I follow her into the dark room, Jocelyn right behind.

"We should light a fire," Jocelyn says.

My mouth opens to respond, but a sickening thump next to me chokes the words in my throat. Before I can process what happened, something hard bashes into my head. The blackened room fills with stars as I sink to the floor.

Chapter
TWENTY-THREE

ༀ

WITH A BUZZING HEAD, I wake. I lay on a hard, uneven floor trying to remember how I got here. A rough rope tightly binds my hands and feet in front of me. The hot room is unnaturally silent, like something waited to pounce on me. The stench of expensive pipe smoke fills my nose, making me want to gag.

While my watering eyes adjusted to the dim light of the fire, I realize Jocelyn is next to me, still. Wanting to make certain she's not seriously injured, I scoot toward my friend. She has to be all right. She just has to.

"I would not do that if I were you." Octavian's voice sends a chill through me, stopping my actions. I turn to glare at him. Emeline stands next to him with a smirk on her face. I stare at her, trying to fathom how she could possibly be here and not tied up.

"Em—Emeline?" My mouth goes dry.

"Ah, yes," Octavian responds. "Emeline has been of great use. Though she would have been more useful if she told that pirate you were pretending to be the human, Adelei."

Emeline's smile turns to a scowl. "I told you, Constance or Stewart was always hovering over me. I never had the opportunity."

"You should have found a way to leave them." His voice is sharp. "The thickheaded pirate couldn't follow orders either. That castle was going to be used for my vacations. I explicitly told them not to destroy anything while they were there. No matter. I'll get what I want out of them. Things have not gone quite as planned, but they will still work out."

"You boar! My parents trusted you. How can you turn on them like this?" I jerk around with the force of my words, but it does no good to my bonds.

Octavian howls, saliva spewing from his gaping mouth. "My dear, it was all too easy. Easier than you'll ever know. And I'm about to be rewarded for my work. I'll begin building my army soon, and then I will attack the humans. It won't be long before I have control of them. I've always wanted slaves at my command. Soon, I will."

"You can't do this! The humans have done nothing to deserve it. You make me sick."

"Nothing? They exist. Every breath they take pollutes the air. You should be grateful that I even allow them to live."

"How can you say that? I've been among some of them. They are no different than elves. They are a better people than you will ever be."

Octavian rests his closed fist under his chin with one finger extended over his cheek. "Some of your fellow elves used to think like that as well. When you were yet a child, about the same time you threw mud at me." His eyes glared at me accusingly. "I started placing rumors of swindling men. I even found men willing to tell other men of the evil nature of elves. It's turned out rather grandly, don't you think? Two nations on the verge of war will be pushed over by the precipice from your broken betrothal."

"Why are you telling me this?" I narrow my eyes at him. If he can tell me all this, what use will he have for me later? My muscles become ridged.

"Husbands and wives don't keep secrets. Besides, I know how much you just *love* your humans. It'll be great for you to have so many of them around all the time. Though I find it quite disgusting that you'd stoop to such a level as to take on their appearance. You're paying for it now, though. Such a shame to waste your beauty. I will miss it."

His words sting my tongue into action. "It's not yours to miss, and it never will be."

"It's time to stop playing these games. You will give into me soon enough."

Octavian brings one finger to his pursed lips and holds it there. I take advantage of his silence to look for means of escape. Shadows from the fire dance across the room, making it so I can't see much. A vague outline of a closed door sticks out but doesn't leave room for hope because Emeline stands in the way. The room has pictures on the wall, though the subjects of which can't be seen in the dim light. Rough, uneven stones are covered a foot from me by a thickly woven rug.

No escape.

I try to keep myself from reaching the despair that's hovering near the edges of my conscious. Now is not the time to give up.

Octavian reaches over to the table next to him, pulling my attention back to him. Grabbing a pitcher, he pours a glass of water and brings it over to me.

"My dear, I know you must be parched in this heat."

Thirsty as I am, I can't bring myself to take a drink from the traitor. The thought sickens me, making my empty stomach roll. When he lifts the glass to my lips, I jerk away.

"I don't want any water from you." I put as much venom in my voice as I can.

Octavian grabs the back of my head and jams the glass to my mouth. He pours the water over my mouth, trying to force me to drink. Instead, it runs down my face and clothes. As he pulls away, I take the little water that made it into my mouth and spit it at him.

Cackling, Octavian throws the glass to the wall. Shards fly across the room. I thrust my body over Jocelyn, shards landing on my backside. Slowly, I turn back to face him. He sits, toying with a jewel on his bloated finger.

"You're more ladylike than this. You'll do as I want, and lucky for you, I'm letting you chose. Completely your choice, My Lady. You may either choose to deny the words you said to your parents of me, or I will start killing. Jocelyn will be the first. It's your choice. Should you pick the easy road, I have a priest waiting on Captain Smythe's ship willing to wed us."

Fear grips my stomach. There has to be a way out of this. But what? I can't let Jocelyn, or anyone else, be killed because of me. Will marrying him bring war or prevent war? I don't know what the right choice is. "You can't do this. Don't start this madness, I beg of you. What can you hope to accomplish by marrying me against my will or killing the people I love?"

"My Lady, I will have power. Everyone will fear me. Everything I have ever desired will be within my reach."

My throat closes up. He will ruin both countries. "I will not allow a man like you to become king."

Emeline smiles. "He will become king, so you may as well get used to the idea. He will do whatever needs be done. I know he will kill anyone you care about, so I recommend staying on his good side."

Octavian's eyes shine with murder, his gaze boring into me. His eyes soften when he looks at Emeline. She blushes, and a giggle escapes her lips. Nausea threatens to overcome me. Seeing her this open to someone is odd, but having it be him? Disgusting.

Octavian's threat dominates my thoughts. I have no idea what he's capable of. The thought of being married to him is intolerable, but what other way is there out of this trap he's placed me in? There has to be a way to escape. A plan, a thought, an idea—anything that would free me and Jocelyn from his clutches.

Octavian stands and gazes at me, eyes twinkling with amusement. He walks over to Jocelyn's still limp form and pulls out a dagger. Horror pounds through me as he puts the blade to Jocelyn's naked throat. Her eyes flutter open and then widen with fear when she realizes a blade is jammed against her neck.

"Don't do this," I say.

Octavian pulls away from Jocelyn. "I can stop. Say you'll marry me, and Jocelyn will be spared."

My heart twists with agony. No matter how much I care about my friend, I can't save her to condemn two entire races. "I cannot."

He thrusts the weapon back toward Jocelyn's neck. Growling, he speaks through clenched teeth. "You can, and you will. I'll draw this out if I have to. She will be tortured and die, unless you agree. Captain Smythe can even be called in. I've seen him in action. His torture techniques are quite refined."

I twist my body away from him, pain wracking through me.

"Don't worry about giving into him, *Princess*," Emeline says. "I never liked Jocelyn anyway."

I spin around to look her in the eye. Anger bites my words. "Why have you become like this? Jocelyn has only ever been kind."

"Your treasured little Jocelyn is of no concern to me. Octavian has opened my eyes to a wondrous plan you will never understand. I'll support him, no matter how he gets there. Then he will give me everything I have been denied by you."

"I never meant to deny you anything. Even if I did, do you really think Octavian will be any better? He's using you, and one day he'll throw you aside like garbage."

Emeline tosses her head away from me, but not before a glint of doubt colors her eyes. A hand grabs me and twists me back toward Jocelyn.

"Enough of this. Decide now," Octavian shouts.

I whisper, "I can't."

Octavian's face pulls into a snarl. "No excuses. Decide now."

The shiny blade slowly turns red, as Octavian pushes it into Jocelyn's neck. Her lips quiver, and she whimpers.

"Jocelyn." My vision turns red at the sight of her blood working its way until it covers everything.

"That's it," he says. "She's gone."

"*No.*" The shriek comes pouring out of me, my body shaking with the violence of my emotions. "Please, stop. I will do it. Please, don't hurt her or anyone else. I'll do what you want."

Octavian pulls the compromised dagger away from Jocelyn and brings it close to my face with a triumphant look. He pulls out a handkerchief and methodically wipes the blade clean. He grimaces at the sodden cloth and throws it onto Jocelyn. She twists her body until the cloth falls to the stones under her.

Emeline snickers, drawing a defiant glare from Jocelyn.

Octavian cuts the rope that ties my hands and feet. While I rub my wrists and ankles, he moves to cut the cords around Jocelyn's feet but leaves the binding around her hands. He sheaths the knife and yanks me to my feet, pulling me close. I cringe away, and he pulls back further in disgust after looking at my face.

Maybe I can use magic to get out of this? But how? I might be able to get out of the ropes, but then what? Throw a wind at him? Not that I could inside, but my mind isn't being more helpful than that.

"Isn't that so much nicer, my ugly dear? Now that we are getting along, we best be off to the ship. We have a wedding to prepare for."

Chapter
TWENTY-FOUR
❧

A NERVOUS LUMP FORMS in my throat as two pirates row the skiff closer to the pirate ship. Though it's still dark outside, the moon lights the unfurled black sails. This is Captain Smythe's boat. Who knows what waits for me here? A wedding I don't want to participate in. Maybe I can get it thrown out since everyone will know I was married on a pirate ship. I can't count on it, though. If I enter this marriage, there's no guaranteeing I'll ever get out of it.

We pull up next to the boat, and a rope ladder swings down to greet us. Jocelyn is pale and shaking. A dried streak of blood on her neck stands out against her pasty skin. She gives me a tentative smile.

Octavian shoves me before I can return the encouragement. "You first, Princess." He gestures up the rope. Gritting my teeth, I climb. My skirts make it hard, but the rope is firm and steady. I put my hand on the railing and move to pull myself up, but dirty hands grab at me, lifting me over.

I shake off the hands once my feet are planted on the deck. The pirates leer at me while I straighten my dress. Soon Jocelyn is hoisted over the railing, followed by Octavian and Emeline. Just when Emeline tumbles onto the deck, footsteps pound toward us.

"Get this ship moving," Octavian orders Captain Smythe, who hasn't reached us yet.

Captain Smythe swaggers over to Octavian. "We aren't leaving yet. Half my crew is still out there looking for *her*, per your wishes."

"Leave them behind. We need to get a move on, now. There's a wedding that needs to take place. I don't know how long it will take for them to notice she's missing, and I'm not sticking around to find out."

"I will not leave my men." Captain Smythe's voice sends a trill of terror through me, even though it's not directed at me. He turns and tramps to his crew, who wait for him a ways off.

"You won't get away with this," Octavian yells after him. "You won't receive another piece of gold from me."

Captain Smythe's body stiffens, but he doesn't turn.

The shade of red on Octavian's face grows deeper. "Never mind. We'll set sail when his men get back. Until then, we have a wedding to prepare for. It will be at dawn, whether or not we've set sail. Emeline, have one of these pirates show you to a cabin and prepare Arabella for our wedding. Make Jocelyn help."

"Yes, my lord."

A pirate, only slightly cleaner than the others, ushers us forward. While we follow the man, Jocelyn clings to my arm. I don't know who's more scared—her or me—I have years more of practice hiding my feelings.

The pirate motions to a room and moves to the side so we can squeeze past. Flinching under his gaze, I skirt past him. The room reminds me of the one I shared with Constance on Captain Zaccheus's ship, but it's less taken care of. The cramped quarters have two beds, both of which hold thin, holey blankets. A small, grimy dresser with a brush, and above it, there is a mirror that barely shows a reflection.

"Get ready. Your dress was brought on board earlier. I'll be back with it momentarily." Emeline leaves the room, slamming the door behind her.

Jocelyn shakes by my side. The dried blood runs across her neck and trails onto the neckline of her dress. My heart constricts as I look at it, though the danger is over for the time being.

"Are you all right?" I ask.

"I—I think so." Her pale face is getting back some of its color.

"Here. Let me heal that for you." I start to reach up, but she stops me.

"You don't have to do that. It isn't more than a scratch. I'd hate for you to waste energy that might otherwise be used to escape. I can't believe we are here."

"I wish we had something to clean the cut with."

"It'll be fine. Having a bit of dried blood on me is the least of our worries right now."

With a quick squeeze around her shoulders, I gingerly sit on one of the beds and motion toward the brush. It at least looks cleaner than anything else in the room. "Let's keep busy. I don't want to anger anyone further. The hostile environment on this boat is like a powder keg, and I don't want either of us to be the one to make it blow."

Jocelyn nods, grabs the brush, and reaches me. She brushes my hair in silence. The air is tense with unease. With each familiar stroke, I become more relaxed.

It must do the same for Jocelyn because she says, "My lady, you mustn't go through with this. He's a madman. Who knows what will happen to your people if you marry him? I've never seen someone so consumed by madness. I admit I'm frightened, but what happens to me doesn't matter."

The pirate standing guard outside the door shifts his weight, reminding us of his presence. Escape that way is not an option, and that leaves only one exit from the room. The sound of water crashing onto the boat plays gently in the background, like music ill suited for the situation.

"If only it were that easy," I say. "I'm afraid of him and what he's capable of. I keep hoping for a chance to escape, but I haven't seen anything that could help us. You're right. He's a madman, and I fear how far he'll go if I refuse him. I know he would have killed you. That can't happen. You are too dear to me." There's no way I could bear to watch Jocelyn be tortured because of me.

She shrugs me off, though not without a quiver to her hand. "I'll die if I must. My life is not nearly as important as yours."

"Don't say that. You are important. I will never forgive myself if I could prevent your death and didn't. You are a true friend. I won't give up on you."

"I'm pleased you think of me as a friend, but it doesn't change the fact that my life, my influence, is meaningless compared to yours. Even more, it means nothing if he's to marry you and gain the throne. He will ruin all that's good." Her chin trembles, but her words hold steady.

"He will. What can I do, though? There are no options left."

"There is one. It may be impossible, but we should at least try."

Surprised at her words, I snap my head up to give her a closer look. "What is that?"

"We could try to escape by—"

Her words are cut short by Emeline's entrance. "I doubt you'll be able to escape what's awaiting you." Emeline sneers at us. "You're on a boat about to set sail. No one here wants to help you. They've all been ordered to keep an eye out, to make sure you don't escape, and you are running out of time. Your wedding will take place just after dawn, which will be arriving shortly."

"You are cruel," Jocelyn says. "Have you no feeling left in your body? I've tried so hard to be your friend, and you rejected that for someone like Octavian? You make me sick."

Emeline smirks. "I never wanted to be your friend. Your constant chatter is enough to drive the sanest person mad. I hope Arabella fights just hard enough for you to have a small taste of torture. It's the way I feel around you."

Jocelyn balls her hands into fists, but I speak before things can become more heated. "I'm cooperating, Emeline, so there is no need to worry about anything happening to Jocelyn. As for you, I'm saddened by your decisions. You're a good person, and I wanted us to be friends. If you were open with me, instead of going to Octavian, we could have resolved our differences. That choice will always be there, but it can't happen unless you abandon this plot."

Emeline struggles for words. "You... I... It— Never mind. Things will happen the way they're supposed to. Lord Octavian has made sure of that. Now, Princess, it's time to get into your wedding gown."

Trembling with anger, I stand and walk over to her. My body is stiff as I try to control myself. "Don't forget my words about Octavian. He will not be as kind to you as I would have been."

I yank the white dress out of Emeline's hands and storm off to the corner—not nearly far enough. The smug look on Emeline's face slips away, replaced with confusion. Her eyebrows knit together for a few moments before she turns and hurries out of the room.

I give a sigh. "I wish I didn't have to put this on," I say.

"Then don't," Jocelyn responds.

If it wasn't for the images of her being tortured flashing through my mind, I wouldn't. "Let's get it over with."

As we work to put on the dress, I can't help but think this isn't how I pictured things going on my wedding day, even if it was to be an arranged betrothal. Once I'm dressed, I frown at the frilly dress. "It's good that I won't wed today." If I can manage to find a plan of escape. "This dress is ghastly. I can't imagine ever getting married in something so distasteful. I look like a lacy mess."

The corners of Jocelyn's mouth move upward. "Emeline doesn't have very good taste, does she?"

We laugh. Emeline never did pick out my clothes, only brought them to me. Our mirth fades as the seriousness of the situation eradicates our congenial mood. Her eyes fill with fear, and I close the distance between us to wrap my arms tightly around her. We embrace like long-lost sisters.

"How can we escape?" I whisper.

"I'm not sure." She ponders, and then says, "Maybe when they take us out, we can both make a break for the railing and jump ship. I could probably swim to shore. Could you make it?"

"Perhaps, but the way we're surrounded, I doubt the opportunity will come."

She gives a solemn nod. "What about magic, then? Is there any way it could help us out of this mess?"

"I don't know. Let me think about it." I study the cabin, wracking my brain for a plan when the door bursts open.

Emeline enters, breaking the moment with a distasteful look on her face. "So sorry to interrupt, but it is time for your wedding, Princess."

I clench my fist as she motions me out the door. Mustering all my strength, I walk into the dawning morning.

Jocelyn starts after us, but Emeline stops her. "Oh, didn't I tell you, Jocelyn? You will be staying here with a guard who's more than willing to dole out punishments for misbehavior. I'd be careful if I were you. I've heard he has a very bad temper." Emeline shoves Jocelyn back into the room, causing her to stumble and fall. Then she shuts the door and locks it.

"You will pay for this someday," I say to her. "I'll see to it."

"Wrong. Everyone else may pay, but Lord Octavian will make sure I'm well taken care of."

"I highly doubt that."

"What do you know?" Emeline's voice grows shrill, the words coming faster as she speaks. "He promised me anything I desired. Riches. Jewels. All the human slaves I want. The only thing I had to do was watch you from the inside and report to him. I've been telling him about your actions for a long time. I've done my part. He'll give me everything I desire. Your parents will be taken care of soon, and then I'm sure I can convince him to destroy you and let me take the throne in your place."

I scoff. "You're delusional. He'll do nothing for you, even if he does win. I'll not let that happen, though. I'll do what I must, and then you'll receive your reward for being a traitor."

"Ah, yes." Octavian's voice startles me. "You have power to do whatever you want, my dear. As soon as we are married, I shall take care of Emeline for you. I believe I know a few places we could send her."

Emeline's jaw drops, and Octavian sneers at her. He shoves my shoulder, pushing me toward the front of the ship while Emeline huffs behind us. His touch is revolting, making me stiffen and pull away. It takes all my power not to run from him. That, and there's nowhere to run to.

The ship is full of pirates. An elven priest shifts nervously in front of Captain Smythe. The captain's face looks as if he could blow up like a volcano, sending the whole ship into the depths of the sea. I make a mental note to stay as far from him as possible.

A flock of seagulls flies overhead. The sun has just peeked over the horizon when Octavian and I stand in front of the priest. The usually filthy pirates are gathered around, looking like they at least attempted to clean up.

My knees are weak as the priest speaks. He looks uncomfortable and keeps mopping the sweat off his forehead, though the air is cool.

I rack my brain but can't come up with any thoughts on how to get Jocelyn and me to safety. I dart my gaze about nervously, looking for something to give me an idea. The priest's mouth is still moving—words are said, but none of them enter my head. I needed a chance to save Jocelyn. There has to be something. It can't end like this.

And then it happens. Out of the corner of my eye, I spot a familiar merchant vessel.

Chapter
TWENTY-FIVE

RABELLA, ANSWER THE priest." Octavian's voice shatters my dream.

My mind races for a way to stall until the ship arrives. "I'm sorry—what was that?"

"You need to answer the priest. Don't go changing your mind now."

"I—I..."

"What? Spit it out, girl."

"It's just that I think maybe this isn't such a good idea."

"Don't start with me." His scowl is deeper than ever.

"I can't do this. I know better than this, and I won't give you what you want."

"You will." His face boils, his voice dangerously low. He grabs my arm, and the pain and pressure make my finger ache. "If you don't do this, I'll get Jocelyn. You'll watch as

Captain Smythe tortures her. Sooner or later, you will give in. I'd recommend doing so before people have to die."

"Why should I give in to you? You might just go ahead and kill them anyway. Anyone who gets in your way is a risk. For all I know, you'll kill me a few years down the road, after you've been crowned king. I'll never give you what you want."

He brings my face to his with a forceful jerk, his rank breath making the contents of my stomach protest. His dark eyes try to pierce through me.

The anger and hatred building within me are horrifying. I try not to let myself tremble, concentrating on the fact that help is coming.

He darts his gaze about, his eyes growing stormier. All of a sudden, the wind picks up, and I know it's him casting a spell. His emotions are getting the best of him. He could destroy us all. Lightning dances in his eyes as the early morning sun is covered by black, angry clouds.

I follow his line of sight to Captain Zaccheus's ship. Robert's ship. My heart feels like it's yanked from me.

The seas become rougher while the angry wind howls. Gathering all my strength, I release my magic from the inside. The light prickles move from my chest to my arms and out of my hands, shooting straight for the sky. The clouds move, letting the sunlight shine through.

Octavian turns his face back to mine, mystified. "You can't be doing this." Shock taints his words. "You already have skills in gardening, and I know of your face transformation. You shouldn't be able to do more than that. At least not to such a strong degree."

I glare and give him my most vicious smile. The wind becomes a gentle breeze, and I release the spell. Octavian snarls and thrusts his arms out in front of him. The light disappears again behind dark clouds. Drops of rain fall on me, quickly turning to a fierce downpour.

I turn toward the sky, wondering how I can possibly combat him when an idea comes to me. I raise my arms above me, and magic races upward through them. I concentrate on the rain, focusing as much of it as I can on Octavian. Chilling the air, I turn the rain centered on him to hail.

As they come swishing down, several bits of hail pelt me with stinging pain, but they are nothing compared to the torrent unleashed upon him.

Lightning flashes, brightening his twisted face. Stunned at the pure hatred it contains, I falter and take a step back. In my short distraction, he pulls himself out of the hail and toward me. He raises his hand and brings it down sharply on my cheek.

Captain Smythe takes notice of the approaching boat and yells orders at his men. The pirates scatter about, swords drawn. The wind whips my hair. The distance between the pirates' ship and Robert's is decreasing rapidly as I send them an aiding wind, ignoring the stinging on my face.

"You will not defy me." Octavian's harsh voice jerks through me.

"I will," I yell back.

He grabs me by the arm and drags me across the ship toward the room Jocelyn is held in, forcing my spell to cease. I kick and scream, but he pulls me along. He's so much bigger than me that I can't get a grip.

Robert's ship pulls up next to the pirates', and men pour aboard. I try to kick my heels into the deck to slow Octavian, but with frightening intensity, he throws me against the door.

I crumple to a heap. Then the pain hits, spreading through every part of me. Where is the guard?

He swaggers forward and stops before reaching me. Seeing him raise his foot, I curl into a ball to protect myself from the blow.

Crash.

I fall backward as the door behind me gives way from his kick. I tumble into the room. He wasn't aiming for me after all. He is more capable than he looks. With pain radiating through me, I frantically search for Jocelyn. All I can find are two bunks and the empty dresser. The room is deserted. Some of the tension leaves, but I can't help but wonder where she is. If she's safe.

Octavian howls. "Emeline, you will pay for double crossing me."

Seeing his wrath heading in my direction, I roll farther out of reach until I bump into the dresser. Within two steps, he catches up to me, lifts his arms, and whips it down full force. I put my arm up to block him the best I can.

A mere second before impact, a massive hand grabs Octavian's arm and throws him to the ground. Captain Smythe looms over us, hatred flowing out of him like molten lava.

"You scoundrel," Captain Smythe bellows. "Trying to make me do all the work and not pay me for it. Now my ship is overrun with humans and elves trying to kill my men. I am done listening to you. I'll tell you what's going to happen. While my men take care of these pests, you will go get my gold, and then I'll leave you on the beach to watch me sail away. Never to ask anything of me again."

Octavian stumbles to his feet before regaining his composure. I try to make myself as small as possible while the two men try to outdo one another. Octavian straightens his back and looks up at Captain Smythe.

Though he's dwarfed by Captain Smythe's height, Octavian doesn't appear worried. His face tightens, and he balls his fists. "Captain Smythe, I do believe I hired you to do an easy enough job, yet you managed to foul it up on every point. There will be no pay unless you finish the job, scumbag."

"Just try leaving the boat alive without giving me what is duly mine."

Octavian tries to move past Captain Smythe to get to me. Captain Smythe doesn't budge, and for once, I'm grateful to him.

"You fool," Octavian says. "With her magic abilities, she'll unleash who-knows-what type of spell on us. We can discuss this later."

His words give me the push to find something I can manipulate to my favor. The wind howls more loudly, and the boat sways harder, back and forth. Though I'm still sitting, the constant rocking makes it difficult for me to think past the churning inside me.

There has to be something that can be used as a weapon or magically enhanced. A few bits of dirt are the only thing on the floor. Nothing on the bed. I don't dare reach for the brush and hair ornaments, but I make note that they're there.

"I will no longer follow your rules, soothsayer," Captain Smythe says. "If you don't give me and my men our pay, I will take the princess with me."

No. Not that.

Octavian's gaze darts about. I shrink back. Neither of these men will bring me anything but harm. I want to rush for the exit, but a man and elf stand in my way.

Both males' bodies teeter with the tossing ship. Lightning flashes through the open door, brightening the space around Captain Smythe's body. Octavian opens his mouth to speak, but before any words come out, Captain Smythe groans in pain and shuffles further into the room, almost stepping on me.

I scurry the other way as another man storms to us.

Robert.

He's covered in sweat and a bleeding wound is on his left arm, but he's come.

"My lady, if you would be kind enough to wait out in the hall, I will safely escort you to shore if one of my men doesn't show up," he says without looking at me.

I rise and head for the door, staying as far from Octavian and Captain Smythe as possible. Robert shifts slightly to make room for me to leave. As I pass, I lightly touch his arm, sending it magical healing energy and renewing him.

Before I make it out of harm's way, Captain Smythe steps forward and swings his sword, hitting Robert on the head with the hilt. He grabs me, pulls me close, and brings his blade to my neck.

Panic threatens to overwhelm me, but I work to stay calm. Robert has an oozing gash on his head, but he doesn't seem to notice as he stares at me wide-eyed. "Let her go," he says.

Captain Smythe sneers. "She's the best bargaining chip there is. I don't think I'll be letting her go. You know, I think I'll be taking Octavian with me. Some of my boys could use some work on their torturing skills."

The blood drains out of Octavian's face as Captain Smythe edges closer, still holding the sword against my neck. My heart races while the boat remains unsteady around us. As we inch closer to the deck, I maneuver my hand, to reach the hairpins on my head. Octavian's face goes from white to green. When we reach him, Captain Smythe withdraws the sword from my neck.

I slip one of the pins into my hand, pull my fist forward, and bring it back down, thrusting the pin into Captain Smythe's leg. As soon as it's in, I cast a spell on the metal, bending it into a hook.

"Stupid wench." Captain Smythe grunts in pain.

He yanks me away from his injured leg and holds me against his other side. He tries to yank out the pin, but despite several swift tugs, it doesn't budge. He clamps his jaw shut and leaves the hook in. He motions Octavian closer with his sword. The movement is slight, but the sword fills the small room with action, whipping around.

Desperate now, I search for anything else I can use to change the odds. A flash of inspiration comes when lightning lights up the room. I scoot my foot backward and touch the plank Captain Smythe is standing on. Magic spreads through me, releasing its energy into the board. Using the spell, I put pressure on the flimsy spots I can find in the boards. With the plank weakened, I pull away, praying it'll work.

Captain Smythe shifts his weight to the foot not on the fragile board. I grit my teeth and lean forward. His weight shifts with my movement, and his massive leg crashes through the floor.

I wrench free of his grasp and attempt to get as far as possible. Octavian stands there, still green, his eyes wide. Robert lunges for the pirate, and Captain Smythe's body crumples in pain from the jagged plank that digs into his leg.

Octavian springs up with Robert focusing on Captain Smythe. Racing to leave the heated room, he bolts for the door that's now unguarded. Robert turns at the noise and thrusts himself forward, barely cutting Octavian off.

Captain Smythe pulls his leg from the hole, blood running down it. He knocks me to the side and barrels to the exit. Colliding with Robert, Captain Smythe bashes Robert's head, opening another wound. Grimacing, Robert raises his sword and swings at Captain Smythe's arm. Octavian cowers in the corner away from the fighting men, and I watch, waiting for an opportunity to help.

Captain Smythe flinches as Robert's sword slices a deep wound on his arm. The pirate thrusts his sword toward Robert, who parries it from entering vital organs but doesn't escape it piercing his side. Robert holds his sword up to fight, but it sways with his taxed body.

Captain Smythe shoves him to the ground and runs for the door. Octavian is about to follow, when I jump toward him and push with all my might. Falling over Robert, Octavian crashes to the floor. He staggers to get up, but I grab

Robert's sword out of his limp hand and hold it to Octavian's jeweled throat.

"You know how well I'm trained with a sword. Do not dare test my patience. Get on the bed now," I say.

"But—"

"Now."

Looking defeated, Octavian sulks to the bed and sits motionless. Another bolt of lightning flashes, and his eyes lose the fire they once held. I keep the sword pointed at him, torn between making sure he does no more damage and going to Robert. A moan from Robert spins me into action.

Watching Octavian, I cut a strip of the bottom of the wedding dress. "Put your hands together by the bunk and don't move." I make quick work of tying his hands together and then run to Robert. I kneel by him and try not to let my emotions overwhelm me. "I'm going to fix you up now."

I look over his wounds as best I can while still keeping an eye on Octavian. Carefully, I place a hand on Robert and try not to lurch with the tossing ship. I cast a healing spell, fearing neither of us has enough health to spare.

The bleeding from all his wounds slows but doesn't stop. The gashes on his head look as if they will heal over time, and with much care, his torso should too. But it's hard not to worry. In a short amount of time, the cabin floor has become slick with his blood.

His eyes flutter.

"Robert, stay with me." A tear slips down my cheek.

He sputters and coughs. In a voice like the whisper of butterfly wings, he says, "Arabella, you're making a good choice in marrying the prince." His eyes fill with peace, and then they close.

"No, Robert. Come back. Don't do this now." I search for the tiniest bit of magic, sending him every last drop of health I can use from my own body. Agony tears through me, cutting me apart I as hold onto his limp form. I put my face down by his cheek, my tears pouring on both of us—though they're not from the physical pain.

It hasn't been long enough for me to know him. He can't die now. Not ever. I wanted to be part of his life, and even though I can't, I want to know he's still out there somewhere living a good life. He can't go like this. He just can't.

Footsteps pound toward us. In hope of help, I ignore the pain and pull away. Abner enters the room. He takes in all the blood and my hand over Robert's wound.

"What have you done to him, witch?" He storms over and pushes me away with a surprising strength. Two more humans enter the tiny room, their eyes widening with horror. "See what this elf has done to him?" Abner says. "I told him these elves weren't to be trusted. Get him to our ship. We have to leave this diabolical place."

"No," I say, my voice pleading. "You have it wrong. I was trying to help him. Please, you must let our healer attend him."

Abner turns and spits on me.

Misery and shock stun me. I can do nothing while the three men carefully pick up Robert's body and edge out the door, their footsteps soon fading in the distance. I try to go after the men, but as soon as I stand, I fall back to the ground, exhausted from use of my magic.

Octavian stands with a smug expression on his face that dissipates when more footsteps come down the hall. As familiar elvish faces come into view, I faint.

Chapter
TWENTY-SIX

❧

I STARE OUT THE window.

A month has passed since that frightful day on the boat. Everything has seemed so distant. Cold and lonely.

Jocelyn enters the room and strolls over to me. "My lady, is there anything I can do for you?"

"No, thank you, Jocelyn. I'm fine." My voice sounds feeble to my own ears.

"All right, my lady."

"I'm sorry. I'm afraid I've been moping again. Perhaps I'll take a walk in the garden or do some fencing."

"Yes. First, the king and queen would like a word with you."

"I'll go see them shortly."

Jocelyn dips her head and moves to leave the room.

"One more thing," I say. "I've told you there's no need to be so formal with me. You may use my name. I'd enjoy your company in the garden this evening, if you wish to join me."

She beams. We've spent much time together in the recent weeks, and though it's hard not to be distant since I'm caught up in the affairs of state and, more importantly, wondering what happened to Robert, the bond between us is strengthening. "Yes, I'd like that. There were new flowers blossoming when I was there this morning. Plus, I saw a few that could benefit from your skills. I'll be there when you're finished." With that, Jocelyn leaves the room.

After freshening up some, I head down to the great hall to meet with my parents. On the way, my thoughts turn to the scroll. Constance informed me that Andries is getting close to making it completely readable. What he's uncovered so far confirmed its authenticity. My parents were right to try to force the marriage. If it came true, it would help both of our races. But after all that's happened, we still don't know if there will be a wedding.

When I enter the grand hall, my parents are on their thrones, and Reginald stands behind them. Though I don't like it, he's taken Octavian's place as one of their advisers.

The thick, red carpet covers the entire stone floor. My bare feet barely make a sound while I walk over to them. Enormous pictures hang on the wall. Most are of my mother, though a few are of me—before the spell's consequence—and some of my father are scattered in between them, along with one of all three of us. Two guards stand at either side of the thrones. The guard is rebuilding, though it will take more time to get their strength back to what it was.

I reach the stairs in front of my parents and curtsy. Mother avoids my gaze, even after all this time. She sits upon her throne, head held high, looking regal as ever. My father is different. He holds my gaze, having adjusted to the differences in my appearance. During the previous weeks, he's taken me more seriously, valuing my thoughts and opinions. No doubt that's why I was called to meet with them—some matter he wants my input on.

The thought flatters me but isn't what I wish for. Peace and respect between humans and elves—that's what's needed.

And Robert. I don't know if he's even alive.

I haven't heard from him since he was carried out of that cabin, though I've sent more than one note inquiring after him.

"Thank you for coming," Father says. "There are a couple items of business I wish to speak with you about. The first concerns Octavian."

I suppress the groan that wants to rise out of me. The filth was nothing but trouble upon his capture. Being the king and queen's aid so long, he knew all the loopholes and wasn't afraid to use them. The hour I was supposed to spend in elven court against him turned into a week, and the experience left me drained and angry. I clench my fists thinking about it.

"I still can't believe it was he who betrayed us," Mother interrupts. "He joined us shortly after your birth. Doubtless if he had been around before, he would have talked us out of ever betrothing you. He convinced us to do so much. I never wish to see that elf again."

Father raises his gaze to the ceiling and lets out a sigh. "Yes, my dear. We will have his treachery taken care of soon enough. As I was trying to tell Arabella—"

"I'm not certain exiling him to the Crimson Ruins is good enough. I still think we should behead him. I can't believe that thing was ever in the same room as me." She gingerly brushes her arm as if to wipe it of any remnants of Octavian.

"As you may have gathered from your mother, the council decided against the death penalty in favor of exile. His days will remain lonely, giving him time to think upon his actions. It is a fitting consequence."

"I agree," I say. "It'd be ill for us to stoop to his level and execute him. Maybe in time he will change his ways, though I for one will always remain wary of his actions."

"Well said." Father nods in agreement. "Emeline's punishment won't be as harsh because of her helping Jocelyn to escape. She's sentenced to help an orphanage in Pomum Heart. She'll be carefully watched over and hopefully can gain a softer heart."

"Yes, I hope the children can thaw her," I say, thinking of the last time I was with the children. They are sweet and kind, if a bit rambunctious at times. If anything can soften her heart, I believe they can. Emeline herself was not unkind last we spoke, though she was very caught up in what was outside her window. "When we last spoke, she was sorrowful. I believe she has a chance."

"She has changed already, but there's still much work to be done," he says. "Now, the second item of business I called you here for—an emissary brought a letter today that concerns you."

I straighten with this news. I didn't expect a reply now of all days. I was beginning to think it would never come. "What did it say?"

"The humans were moved by the words you urged us to send them. They understand the circumstances and are willing to take us up on the offer. The betrothal is restored, and the wedding will take place once the appropriate arrangements have been made."

Reginald speaks for the first time, his eyebrows drawn together. "Yes, they have been quite understanding."

Closing my eyes, I try to keep my face smooth. So it will take place. Robert's final words spring to mind. *You are making a good choice in marrying the prince.* I strengthen myself with the memory.

I open my eyes and force myself to ask about the second item I inquired about. "And Robert? What of him?"

For the first time, Father's gaze darts to the floor. I clench my jaw and try to remain steady while he struggles for words. Pain hovers over me, ready to swoop in with the wrong words.

"*No.*" Mother's voice is shrill, making the pain jump in but not in the way I expected. "I cannot allow our daughter to be so caught up with a common sailor. I will not have it."

I open my mouth to defend myself, but my father surprises me by saying, "Pernilla. That common sailor—as you put it—has done more for our family than we will ever be able to repay." His gaze shifts to me, filled with compassion, and his voice softens. "I'm afraid we'll not be able to even try, though. Arabella, I'm so sorry. He passed from this world shortly after the ship left."

My heart feels odd. Almost as if someone stands in front of me and tries to rip it from my chest. More words are said, but they have no meaning. The pain is brutal. I'm vaguely aware of being dismissed by my father and traversing through the halls out of the castle. I wander to a deserted place in the garden and fall into a heap on the grass.

There should be tears—I know there should, from the pain hewing me in two—but none come. My body is lifeless and heavy with the sun blaring down upon me. The images around me shudder. My thoughts creep to my time with Robert. The simple feel of his warm touch against my skin. The way his golden-brown eyes locked with my gaze. His caring— *No*. I can't allow myself to go further.

The anguish slicing through me is worse than anything I've yet to experience. I gasp for breath and suck in something salty. I reach a dirty hand up to feel my face. A strange realization overcomes me.

I'm sobbing.

That's why the world appears to shake around me. It's not the world; it's me. The thought makes the tears come on more fiercely.

A hand gently touches my shoulder. I want to ignore it. To ignore the all of Omanska. But I can't. I am their princess.

I look up to find Jocelyn bending over me. Her green eyes sparkle with tears as well. I shift toward her as she sits next to me. We lean on each other for support while the tears run their course.

The pain doesn't lessen. It still eats at me, threatening to rip me apart, but Jocelyn is here to hold me together. Her presence makes it easier to bear.

The sun moves across the sky while I cry. The tears eventually ease, and she pulls out a handkerchief for me. Embarrassed but grateful, I accept it and dry my eyes and nose.

"I know it doesn't mean much, but I'm sorry." Her words are soft.

"It does mean something to me. I'm being silly anyway."

She shakes her head. "No. We all saw how you two cared for one another. It would have been hard to miss. Though it was an impossibility for you two to be together, you shouldn't have to lose him like this."

I bite my bottom lip in an attempt to hold back the tears again.

After several minutes, Jocelyn speaks again. "I'm sorry for the way things are. Though I can't fully understand how you're feeling, I do wish things were different. Unlike you, I'm not bound to marry someone I don't know, but I'm unable to marry at all while in your service. I don't wish to leave you, but my heart aches for what I saw between you and Robert."

"I had no idea."

"I'm not trying to complain. Maybe I'm out of line, telling you this. I hope to find someone like Robert someday. He was good to us all."

"Yes. He was kind. Though I suppose that's an understatement. I'll always remember him and strive to be like him." Tears splash down my cheeks again.

Jocelyn laughs, startling a flock of nearby birds into flight. "I don't think you can get any kinder, my lady. It's hard to find a selfish act coming from you."

"Please, call me Arabella." I smile through my tears. "And I do think I can be kinder. In fact, there's something I know

I can change. We will get rid of the law prohibiting you from courting. I won't let you fall to the same fate as Constance in the matters of love. Besides, one of us ought to find our mate and be able to spend our life with him. You will be my new hope for true love."

"My lad—Arabella, I don't know what to say."

I laugh. The sound feels strange next to the pain in my heart. "Thank you is enough. Still, I should thank you. This will give me something happy to cling to."

"Thank you. Though it doesn't begin to cover it."

"It will more than cover it." I feel lighter already. We embrace like the two sisters we've become.

Chapter
TWENTY-SEVEN

ᵔᵔ

M Y WHITE DRESS is adorned with small dia-
monds. It reaches the floor, hiding my bare feet,
and trails behind me. A sheer white veil attaches
to my crown and covers my face. I've always expected this
moment to be a happy one. That somehow the betrothal
would be broken and I'd marry someone I loved.

Maybe even Robert.

It's foolish to allow such dreams.

How my heart aches.

Holding back tears, I glance at the door and steel myself
for what's to come. Soon one of the servants will be coming to
say it's time to get married. Then I'll go to the hill, where everyone is waiting. It's been lavishly decorated with blooming
flowers. Many people will be there, both humans and elves,
wanting to see if our two races will really unite by marriage.

As my thoughts wander, Constance appears at the door. A smile dances on her lips, though it doesn't reach her eyes. "My dear, Arabella." She walks over and places a hand on my check. "I know this isn't what you wanted, but you're doing the right thing."

"Thank you. That means a lot, coming from you," I say.

"My dear, they are all waiting for you."

She leads me from the room, out of the castle, and up the hill toward the forest. Feelings threaten to overcome me, so I look to the ground, trying to keep my balance.

As we reach the crowd, Constance says, "I'm going to my place up front." She smooths out my dress. "Oh, my dear." She gives my arm a squeeze and then is gone to meet me at the head of the aisle.

After several long, deep breaths, I start the long walk. Everyone stands when I approach. There's so many of them. Too many. I hold my head high but keep my gaze on the ground. The only sound reaching my ears is that of birds, singing their sweet song. As my bare feet land on the soft, white flower petals, I ready myself to meet my future husband for the first time.

My thoughts stray to Robert and the time we spent together. Deep down, I felt a strength in him I hope to draw from now, even if I'll never see him again. The memory of his words and actions will see me through this. It's what he'd want me to do.

While I continue forward, I try to think of my people. Of what I'm doing this for.

The end of the aisle arrives too quickly, but peace settles through me. Prince Phillip has brightly polished shoes. They remind me of the dream I had, so long ago, but this won't end in a nightmare. I won't let it. Peace settles through me. Robert approved of this. Prince Phillip and I will end the conflict between elves and humans.

I stop and hands I know to be Constance and Jocelyn both move to lift the veil. I follow it with my gaze, looking at the prince's well-tailored clothes up to his broad shoulders.

With a pounding heart, I look into a face that's familiar. "Abner?"

"I'm sorry about everything." Though his words are contrite, his face is puckered like he doesn't want to be saying them.

How can this be? Why would he be here, an elf-hating human such as him. "What are you doing here?"

"I'm Prince Phillip. There'll be time to talk later, but I—"

"Wait, there won't be time to talk later because we'll be married. Everything will be said and done by then. You better explain yourself now."

He darts his gaze to the ground before meeting mine again. "The most important thing for you to know is that I lied."

"Of course you lied." I keep my voice down, despite wanting to yell. "That much is obvious. What exactly are you getting at?"

"Don't you see him? Robert. He's alive, standing behind me."

I search with my gaze, and my chest lifts. Can it really be? Is he alive?

And then I see him. Robert, his golden brown eyes gazing at me. He's alive.

And I'm about to marry his best friend.

about the
AUTHOR
∽

A MAZON BEST SELLING author Janeal Falor lives in Utah with her husband and three children. In her non-writing time she teaches her kids to make silly faces, cooks whatever strikes her fancy, and attempts to cultivate a garden even when half the things she plants die. When it's time for a break she can be found taking a scenic drive with her family, fencing, or drinking hot chocolate.

SIGN UP TO RECEIVE RELEASE NOTIFICATIONS AT:

www.janealfalor.com

ACKNOWLEDGEMENTS

I WANT TO GIVE a big thanks to the people who made this book possible. It takes a lot of work to make a book and without these people, this book would still be a sad, lonely little draft. Having said that, whatever faults are left, are purely my own. I know they would be many, many more were it not for the help of these people.

I huge, appreciative high five goes to Callie Chinen, for not only beta reading, but doing so on a very ugly draft. She helped me from the get go, and her positive feedback kept me going. I'd also like to thank Wil Scott and Marie Krepps for beta reading for me. Your input was invaluable.

A thank you to Tracey Joesph for reading through a later version of the book and helping me fix so many third person errors, among so many other things. It was a hard decision to change from third person to first person and left many mistakes. I'm so grateful for her help finding them.

Thank you to my copy editor, Sotia Lazu. She's amazing at cleaning up my manuscripts and helping me find things I'd never even thought of before. She's my superwoman/editor. And thanks to Yesenia Vargas for proofreading for me. It's a messy job and she makes good work of it.

As always, a massive thanks to my family for not just allowing me to work, but cheering me on. Tai, thanks for telling everyone we meet, even grocery store clerks, that your mom writes. A special thanks to my husband, Erik, on this one. He read this when it was still the first book I had ever written, the first draft at this. It was horrible, mucky reading, but he guided me and encouraged me through all of it. I love you!

Thanks goes to Karen C. Eddington, who without this book and series would not be possible. She cheered me on from the moment she read and continued to tell me how excited she was about the book when I was working on something else. She always encouraged me to come back to it, and I'm so glad she did. Thank you, sis!

And thank you reader, for following along Arabella's story. Without you, there would be no point to writing at all.

www.ingramcontent.com/pod-product-compliance
Lightning Source LLC
Chambersburg PA
CBHW060316260626
47160CB00007B/2628